Caught

She went to the locker to get her white coat. She could see Gary in the back of the pharmaceutical vault. "Hi," she called as she was buttoning her jacket.

You'd have thought that she'd shot him in the back, he jumped so high. He turned toward her as she was coming into the vault. "God, you scared me." He was angry. "Knock first. Okay? This is pretty concentrated work."

"Sorry. I came to help."

"Well, I don't need any help." Was he swaying a little? He looked sort of pasty and pale.

"You sure?" There were little piles of drugs on the counter. It looked like there was a lot of work to do. She moved closer to the counter. "I'm a quick learner. Just show me what to do."

**Other Point paperbacks
you will enjoy:**

The Edge
   by Jeanne Betancourt

The Changeover
   by Margaret Mahy

Roses
   by Barbara Cohen

Last Seen on Hopper's Lane
   by Janet Allais Stegeman

Lure of the Dark
   by Sarah Sargent

Anna to the Infinite Power
   by Mildred Ames

point

BETWEEN US

Jeanne Betancourt

SCHOLASTIC INC.
New York Toronto London Auckland Sydney

ISBN 0-590-33323-2

12 11 10 9 8 7 6 5 4 3 2   6 7 8 9/8 0 1/9

Printed in the U.S.A.   01

Many thanks to James E. Sok, R.Ph., for technical assistance.

For my sister,
Teri Granger

Week One

Chapter 1

"Get up and cheer, good people. It's seven-thirty A.M. — time for another bright, sunny-side-up morning with Jay Towers. We're gonna start the day with the towering top ten, but first the news."

Christine automatically reached over and turned the volume down on the clock radio. The phony, faceless voice continued a few decibels lower.

"What time do you have to be at the hospital?" Carolyn asked as she got out of bed and padded to the closet for her robe.

"Nine o'clock." Christine jumped out of bed, too, and grabbed her robe from the floor where she'd dropped it the night before. She shook it and put it on.

Carolyn was peering into their closet. "There's nothing to wear. Everything's dirty or at the cleaners."

Christine, coming up to her sister, riffled through the rack. "I'd better wear a skirt and heels. Looks professional for the first day on the job."

"A skirt? We ... I ... have gym today."

Carolyn and Christine turned toward one another, their identical light blue terry cloth robes tied around their identical waists. They looked into identical eyes on identical faces. Nothing was said about this first real separation from one another after sixteen years of constantly being together. Not out loud anyway.

In school, on the tennis court, behind the counter at the ice-cream parlor on the Cape last summer — always together. Identical. They even took the same classes at high school. Then the Career Seminar class was divided in half to allow students to take alternate six-week periods at a real job. Mr. Bronstein went "One, two, one, two," all the way up his alphabetical list of kids' names. Carolyn was a "two." Christine was a "one." And Mr. Bronstein was inflexible. This meant that for the last three months of their junior year they wouldn't be going to school together. A first.

"Why don't you take the first shower," Christine offered. "You have to leave before me. I'll figure out which tweed skirt and blue sweater is cleaner. That should look professional enough. Don't you think?"

"Don't worry about it," Carolyn said, crossing to the bathroom. "They'll probably give you one of those neat white coats to put over it anyway."

Half an hour later Christine was in a skirt and Carolyn in jeans, each wishing she was dressed like the other. Each a little nervous that they weren't dressed exactly alike.

Christine studied Carolyn's loose brown shoulder-length hair. "Pull the hair back." They did it in unison. Christine studied the effect on Carolyn. They used each other as a mirror. "I think I'll wear it back today. They'll probably make me anyway. Isn't that one of the hygiene things in a hospital?"

"I'll wear mine back, too," Carolyn said, as she searched their cluttered bureau top for matching barrettes.

By eight-fifteen their mother had left for her teaching job, and Carolyn was racing down the block toward the waiting school bus. Christine watched Carolyn from her place at the kitchen table. It felt like a piece of her was being wrenched away. She'd had this lonely feeling before — of being in one place while her twin was in another. She suddenly remembered. When they were in the first grade. She'd gotten the flu a day before Carolyn. Her mother took a sick day from school in order to take care of her. She remembered throwing up the warm ginger ale she'd been given to settle her stomach, and watching soap operas and game shows all day from the couch. When Carolyn got home from school she immediately put on her pajamas, too, and climbed on the couch next to her

4

sick sister. During a *Gilligan's Island* rerun Carolyn threw up all over the quilt that their mother had put over them. Even though Christine got better a day before Carolyn, she told her mother she felt "So sick, mommy, I'm not better at all." She didn't want to have to go to school without Carolyn. And she didn't.

Now she watched the school bus doors close and it drove away with Carolyn.

In the hospital parking lot Christine started to pull her mother's car into one of the spaces that said VISITOR, then backed up and moved into one closer to the hospital that was marked STAFF.

She looked in the rearview mirror for a final check on her makeup before getting out of the car.

As she pushed herself through the revolving doors into the hospital lobby, she took a deep breath. She loved the clear, clean, antiseptic smells of a healing place. Most people hated the smell of hospitals, but she loved it the way a painter loves the smell of paints. Was that so weird? She knew from the first time she saw reruns of *Marcus Welby* that she wanted to be a doctor when she grew up. Well, looks like this is grown-up time, she thought, as she shared the elevator with two doctors in their faded surgical greens, and a white-clad nurse pushing an intravenous therapy pump.

The elevator stopped at the basement. As

Christine stepped forward to leave through the silently opening doors, one of the doctors scolded her. "Miss, this is the basement. There are no patients on this floor."

She smiled back at him as she walked through the doors into the corridor. "I work in the pharmacy."

He responded with a scowl and a "Humph."

As the elevator doors closed she could read his name on the blue-and-white plastic name tag. I'll steer clear of Dr. Pisinelli, she thought.

The pharmacy was to the right at the end of the long hall, beyond the suite of X-ray rooms. The sign with the arrow going to the left said CAFETERIA. It registered with Christine. Convenient, she thought.

She brushed her skirt with her hand and rubbed back a stray clump of brown hair that had made its way out of the barrette. She rapped gently on the bright blue metal door. PHARMACY. PERSONNEL ONLY the black-lettered sign warned.

She could hear voices on the other side of the door. "Do you think you can manage to get off your behind and come over here and do some picking?" a woman's voice asked.

"I'll do it when I'm good and ready," a male voice answered.

Christine knocked louder.

"Come in," the woman called out. Christine opened the door and walked in. A good-looking, middle-aged woman was standing at a counter, switching little drawers filled with pills with the empty drawers in a cart next to her. She could have been one of her mother's friends — beauty-parlor-curled blondish hair, a little heavy in the hips, bright pink lipstick, and aqua eye shadow. She'd probably been wearing the same shade for twenty years.

The woman looked up from her work. "Hi. What can I do for you?"

"Ah. I'm Christine Baird." Had they forgotten she was starting today?

A desk chair rolled out from behind a seven-foot partition, and a good-looking guy leaned back in it to get a better look at her. "What can we do for you?"

"I'm from Kennedy High. I'm the high school intern. I spoke with Mr. Thompson."

The woman put down the blue drawer and extended her hand to Christine. "I'm Gloria Manor, the staff pharmacist. Alan mentioned you to me last week. He's in IV Therapy. I'll go tell him you're here." She turned to the young man with a lilt of victory in her voice. "Could you finish this up, Gary? I'll be right back." Then to Christine, "Come on. You might as well come with me and get the grand tour at the same time."

The young man got up and extended his hand to Christine. "I'm Gary Sanders. Staff Slave. Nice to meet you." He had a warm, firm handshake. Christine's hands were clammy with anxiety. She wished she'd wiped them on her skirt before she shook Mr. Gary Sanders' hand. He must have noticed. Clammy like a snake. *Yuch.*

"I'm going to start the control drugs," Gary said to Gloria. "You can finish the unit orders when you get back."

Gloria let out a sigh. "That one," she said as they started down the hall, "is a boy wonder."

"Oh?" Christine said, to invite some more information.

"You come from Kennedy. You don't recognize him?"

"I just moved here this fall. Why? Is he special or something?"

"I don't happen to think so, which puts me very much in the minority around here. You'll have to decide for yourself."

Two nurses came off the elevator and headed toward them. "Morning, Mildred; Louise," Gloria greeted them. "This is Christine — " She looked to Christine to finish the introduction.

"Baird," she offered, "Christine Baird. I'm a high school intern."

"Right. Christine, this is Mildred Lerner and Louise Guyette. They work in IV Therapy, mixing all the intravenous admixtures or solutions for the hospital."

The four of them went into the small IV Additive room together. A tall, gray-haired man mumbled hello. He looked questioningly at Christine. "The intern, from the high school," Gloria explained.

"Oh, yes. I interviewed you in January."
He extended his hand and they shook hello.
"Nice to have you. I'm sorry, I don't remember your name."

"Baird. Christine Baird."

"Yes. Of course." He turned to one of the nurses. "Mildred, Connors is out again today, so I'll work with you this morning. Gloria, let Christine stick with you for the next couple of days. Figure out what she can do to help. Gary's really loaded up; maybe assign her to him." He turned back to Mildred, who was laying out bottles of drugs.

"Let's go," Gloria said. "You can help me get the order out to the nurses' stations."

"Gloria, be sure you don't have her working with the control drugs. I don't want trouble from the school," Thompson said, without looking up from his work.

"What are control drugs?" Christine asked as they walked back to the pharmacy.

"Addictive drugs. Morphine, valium, amphetamines. They're kept in a vault. Like jewels." They were back in the pharmacy. "That's what Gary's doing now. He's in the vault counting out the control drugs. We'll send them up to the units this afternoon. They're kept separate from the other drugs. Even on the hospital floors. Why don't you get a white jacket." She looked Christine up and down. "You look like a size medium. The locker's on your right. Across from the vault. That's where the bathroom is, too."

Christine walked past four long rows of

small blue plastic drawers hung above the pill counter. To her left there were three desks, separated by seven-foot-tall partitions. A closed door at the end of the pharmacy was marked MR. A. THOMPSON. Next to Thompson's office the vault door stood opened. It looked like the safe in a bank. Giving a side glance into it as she turned toward the locker, Christine half expected to see stacks of green bills. Instead there were jars of varying sizes, and clear plastic packets containing the bright-colored pills. At the back end of the vault she could see Gary hunched over a small counter.

Christine opened the locker and flipped through the row of hanging jackets. She pulled out a medium and kept up the search until she found a second medium. She was holding the coat hangers in front of her before she realized what she was doing — getting a lab coat for Carolyn, too! She put on one coat and put the other back. Fitting her hands neatly into the pockets, she turned to go back to Gloria at the drug counter.

"Looks good on you."

She jumped at the sound of Gary's voice. He stood at the vault entrance, casually leaning against the door jamb.

"Looks real good."

"Thank you."

"What'd Thompson tell you to do?"

"Help Gloria," she lied. She didn't know why she said that when she knew that

Thompson had suggested she work with Gary. She blushed.

"I'll be over there." He pointed to the desk area closest to Thompson's office. "Working on the computer."

"Computer?"

"Yeah." He closed the day gate on the vault and locked it with a key. "Thompson believes in new technology. We are modern and up-to-date."

"What does it do for you?" she asked.

"All our orders are stored in here. Our control drug usage reports go into it. So does a record of each patient, so we can double-check any potential drug interactions. Most everything we used to do on paper goes into the computer. And more."

"I'd like to see how it works."

She was sorry she'd lied about who she was supposed to work with. She'd much rather work at the computer than count pills. Now it would be up to Gloria to turn her over to Gary.

She went back to the drug counter. She picked drugs and matched them with the nurses' records as she grouped a twenty-four hour supply in each patient's drawer. The drawers replaced the empty ones in the unit carts. When the first two carts were finished they delivered them to the nurses' stations. Gloria taught her the floor plan of the building as they went along.

*   *   *

"The day went by so fast!" she told Carolyn when they were getting ready for bed.

"A lot faster than Mr. O'Brien's American history, I bet."

Christine jumped in under the covers. "I'd love to know more about Gary. He must have been some big deal at school."

"What's his last name again?"

"Sanders."

Carolyn sat down on the edge of her twin's bed. She had the excited grin of an accomplice. "I'll go to the library tomorrow and look him up in the old yearbooks. How's that?"

Christine grinned back. "Terrific."

During her break the next morning, Christine went over to Gary's desk. She'd listened enviously all morning to the beeps of the programs and Gary's tat-tats on the keyboard.

"Hi," she said to his back.

He turned and looked up at her. She was right. His eyes were blue-gray, which was unusual with black hair. "Hello to you. Gloria driving you crazy yet?"

"No. I'm on a break. Do you have time to show me how you use the computer?"

"Sure. Pull over a chair."

She dragged an orange plastic chair next to his and sat down. He moved over so she could see the screen.

"Watch." He entered, Mr. Rios. 50 Mg. DILAUDID Q 4H PRN. "That means the doctor prescribed fifty milligrams of Dilaudid every four hours."

"What's Dilaudid?"

"A morphine derivative, a pain killer. Watch the screen. I press RETURN, and see what happens."

They listened to the whir of the computer. "The computer is comparing this order with the drugs Mr. Rios's been using since he entered the hospital and with his entire medical history. It also compares it with the information we've stored in the program about possible adverse effects and drug interactions."

By the time Gary had finished his explanations, the computer warned, DILAUDID OVERDOSE. FATAL. ADMINISTER 10 MILLIGRAMS OR LESS Q 4 H PRN.

Christine sat on the edge of her seat and stared at the monitor. "My God, look at that. A doctor ordered a dosage that could kill the patient!"

"Gee," Gary said as he leaned back and smiled smugly. "Good thing I'm here."

She studied him for a second. "You're pulling my leg, aren't you?"

"Well, actually the doctor only ordered 5 milligram doses. We wrote in 50 milligram doses . . . for the demonstration." He nudged her ribs with his elbow. "Just wanted to make sure you were paying attention."

She sat back and looked at him. Pretty cocky. "What else do you do on the computer?"

He pulled out a computer disc from the shelf next to his desk. "Inventory. We keep a record of our drug stock. How much we purchased, how much we've used, what's left. That sort of thing."

"I love it."

"You do?" he asked incredulously.

"Yeah. I do." Was she blushing again? "I took some courses at school."

"Glad to hear that." Alan Thompson had come in behind them. "Gary could use some help," he said. He patted Gary on the shoulder. "Afternoons Christine can help you out here, Gary. That way I can use you for some of the other work."

Was Christine being paranoid or did Gary tense up when he heard Thompson's order?

"Sure," Gary said. "Glad to have a pretty girl along."

Thompson smiled broadly. He turned toward his office. "That's our Gary — handsome and harmless."

Chapter 2

As Christine pulled the car into the garage, Carolyn came running from the kitchen. She was madly waving a photocopied sheet. "Read all about it, read all about it!" she yelled through the windshield.

Christine turned off the motor and jumped out.

"Read all about what?" A warm feeling flooded her. A completeness that had been missing during the day — her second day without her twin, her other.

Carolyn grinned excitedly. "The latest, the greatest, the biggest scoop of the century. Yearbook tells all."

Christine grabbed for the paper. "Lemme see."

Carolyn backed up the stairs, the photocopy behind her back. "No. Guess."

So they played the game.

They sat across from one another at the kitchen table — eye to eye, mind to mind. The photocopy from the yearbook was turned upside down in front of Carolyn.

"Carolyn, pay attention," Christine scolded. "You're thinking about something else."

Carolyn sat up straighter and shook her loose hair. "Okay. I'm ready. What was he voted by his classmates?"

"Most popular?" Christine guessed.

"Right."

"And he was a big athlete ... ah ... basketball."

"Right. What about favorite musical group?"

Christine strained her mind toward her sister's. This was tougher. Was it because they hadn't been together all day and had been doing such different things?

"Musical group. Something weird, offbeat," she tried.

"You got it. The Purple Panics."

"I never heard of them."

"I haven't either. But Gary Sanders was wild about them. How about ambition?"

"Make a million."

"Close. 'Make a billion.'"

Christine was tired. From her day at work, from the game. "Now can I see?" she asked as she reached for the photocopy. Carolyn turned the page over and shoved it in front of Christine.

Gary Sanders, his hair longer, grinned at her. He was hanging upside down from the limb of a tree. "Hang loose," stated the caption. His favorite quote was from the lyrics of a song by The Purple Panics. "We travel here but once or twice. Have your fun at any price."

"Is he still that cute?" Carolyn asked. Christine righted Gary by turning the page upside down. The same mischievous grin, the same good build. But he definitely looked better with short hair and right side up.

"He's improving with age," she said.

"You have a crush on him?"

"Nah. Just curious."

"Oh, I see," Carolyn answered. "And when your curiosity is satisfied?"

"Then we'll see," she said.

What Christine liked best about her job so far was delivering the carts to the nurses' stations. The next day she did it alone for the first time. It's different being in a hospital as a worker, she thought. You feel so helpless when you're a patient or a visitor. But now I'm doing something to help and it feels good. It feels right.

"Has the pharmacist gotten here with the cart yet?" Dr. Pisinelli was asking the Orthopedic nurse.

"Right behind you, Doctor," she told him.

As Pisinelli turned toward Christine, he asked, "Can you tell me which cephalosporin antibiotic has the lowest minimum inhibitory concentration against staphylococcus epidermidis?" All without looking up from the medical chart that he was studying.

Christine's mouth fell open. What was he

talking about? How on earth was she supposed to know this stuff? He looked at her directly. "Well?"

"I don't know," she said.

"Who are you?" he bellowed.

"Christine Baird. I'm a high school intern in the pharmacy."

"High school! Nurse, what the hell is a teenager doing delivering drugs?"

But the nurse was gone and Christine had to face a Pisinelli tirade alone. Delivering drugs to the floors might not be so much fun after all.

When she told Thompson what had happened, he said, "Forget it. Pisinelli's always in a state about one thing or another. If he's got a question he can come down here or pick up a phone."

That afternoon she worked at the computer, entering inventory data.

Her heart popped into her throat when a hand tapped her on the shoulder. She looked up.

It was Gloria. "Sorry. Didn't mean to scare you," she said. "But it's the phone. For you."

Was something wrong at home? With Carolyn? As she went to the phone, she had the fear-feeling that she always got when she heard the fire trucks and wasn't at home to be sure everything was safe.

"Hello," she said into the receiver.

"Hi, C. Is it okay to call you like this?" It was Carolyn.

" I guess. Is everything alright?"

"Sure. It's just I have to ask you something."

She relaxed. She knew everything was alright. "What is it?"

"C. It's well, Bob Connell asked us . . . me . . . out."

Bob Connell! When they first came to Kennedy High they'd agreed he was the very best-looking, nicest guy in the school. They'd even fantasized about how great it would be if he were identical twins himself. Two of him would be just right. But there was only one and that one had asked Carolyn out.

"Bob Connell. That's terrific. So what's the question?"

"Should I go?"

"Of course you should!" Christine concentrated. What was really going on here? Then she realized Carolyn felt funny about going on a date without her. They'd never had steady boyfriends. A double date now and then. Hanging out with friends. But neither of them had really had a boyfriend.

"You think so?"

"Yeah."

"It's Saturday night. I guess we'll go to a movie. What will you do?"

Thompson walked past her and gave her a quizzical look over his glasses that said, "Are we going to have teenage telephone time in the pharmacy now?"

"I've got to get off the phone, C.," she whispered into the receiver. "But listen, don't worry about me. I'll go to Linda's party. It's

19

no big deal. Bob Connell! See ya tonight."

They hung up.

Dressed identically, going separate ways. Their mom was dropping Christine off at Linda's and Carolyn off at the Mountain Café, where she was meeting Bob.

"Why isn't he picking you up here?" Christine asked when they were waiting in the car for their mother. "He's got a motorcycle, doesn't he? And it's a nice night."

"It's weird, isn't it? You know this might be our only date."

"Because he's not picking you up? Listen, lots of guys'd rather meet you someplace so they don't have to deal with your parents."

"It's not Mom. It's us — I mean you. He doesn't want to see us together. He says it confuses him. In fact he would have asked us — me — well, one of us out before if there had been only one of us."

"Oh." Christine had to think about that.

"So, I guess if I'd done the first internship he would have asked you out. He was, like, waiting for one of us to leave."

"Weird."

"Definitely. That's why this might be our one and only date. I mean, if he can't deal with us, he can't deal with me. Right?"

"I guess."

Linda's was packed. The kind of party everyone was invited to — popular or not. "Just fill the place," was Linda's motto. Her parents didn't mind a bit. They had a huge loft area in their converted barn. The beamed ceiling was at least two stories high and there was a fireplace big enough to be a walk-in closet. Tonight there were two kegs of beer in it.

Being at a party alone was different from being at work alone. At work she'd only been known as a single. At the party everyone knew her as one of the twins. But which one? She'd only been there an hour and was already sick to death of people saying, "Which one are you?" Or calling her C.C. to be sure they didn't make a mistake. It happened all the time and she usually didn't mind. But without Carolyn there, it was really bugging her.

Dancing was fun, though. One of the electronic wizards from the freshman class was doing a bang-up job with the deejaying. For Christine, dancing was the best part of a party and Joe Trono was a good dancer. "How's your job going?" he asked, when they stopped to catch their breath.

"Alright. I like it."

Mike Cioffi had come up to them with some beers. "What'd you get anyway? For a job?"

"The hospital pharmacy."

Mike was the senior class character and just about everybody's best buddy. "Drugs, drugs, drugs. You gonna get some for me, baby?" He put his arm around Christine's waist. "Wanna dance? This could be the beginning of a great relationship."

Mike was not a good dancer, but he gave it his all and didn't care that he wasn't good. The rest of the party she danced with Mike or Joe or both of them at the same time, so she didn't hesitate to take a ride home with them. Joe drove. Mike seemed more than a little smashed on pot and beer and who knew what else. It was so hard to tell with Mike because he kidded around so much.

"Whaddaya say, Chris?" he asked as they pulled away from Linda's and onto Route 41. "You get the drugs from the hospital. I'll sell them at school. We'll be rich in no time."

"Sure," Christine laughed. "We can use the dough to buy truckloads of those cute striped pajamas for our long jail terms."

"Scaredy-Cat."

When they pulled up to the house a few minutes later, Christine noticed that the light was on in her mother's bedroom but not in her room. Mom was home, but Carolyn wasn't.

" 'Night, guys," she said, as she hopped out.

" 'Night, Chris." Joe leaned out the window. "I was wondering. When you finish your six weeks at the hospital, will your sister go to work and you come back?"

"Yeah."

"Good," he said.

He's awfully cute, she thought.

They waited until she'd gone in before pulling away from the curb.

Fifteen minutes later Christine was sitting up in bed looking through old magazines, waiting for Carolyn. At a minute before one o'clock, their curfew, she heard Bob Connell's Honda roaring up the block.

Carolyn was flushed and smiling when she came in the room. Her hair fell in knotted strands around her face. "I need to wear a scarf on the cycle," was the first thing she said.

She said a lot more as she sat cross-legged in front of Christine on her bed while Christine untangled her hair with a big toothed comb and her fingers.

"He's as nice as we thought. . . . Did you know he's a great dancer? . . . I mean we didn't go dancing, or anything, but we danced in the parking lot. Just a little 'cause our — I mean yours and mine — favorite song was playing in the diner and we could hear it. And he likes all sorts of outdoors stuff like we do. I think I should see him again, don't you?"

"Of course you should, silly," Christine said. "I mean, you'd tell me to do the same thing if the shoe was on my foot. Right?"

Carolyn turned toward her, all smiles, her hair untangled. "Right."

Am I really that beautiful? Christine wondered as she admired her sister, her mirror. Or is she prettier now that she's found a boyfriend?

"Girls!" their mother was shouting. "Wake up!" Christine and Carolyn sat up with a jolt. Carolyn took a quick look at the clock.

Eight o'clock. On a Sunday morning. Was their mother crazy?

Their mother stood there in her nightgown. Tears rolling down her face, looking frantic. "It's awful. Just awful."

"Mom, my God, what is it?" Christine asked.

"Who did you come home with, from the party last night? Who?" Now she sounded angry.

"Joe Trono and Mike Cioffi. I told you when I came in. Why? What's wrong?"

She pulled Christine to her in a desperate hug. "Oh, my God. My babies. To think you could have been in that car."

Carolyn was on Christine's bed, too. "Mom, what is it?"

She didn't let go of Christine when she told them. "Those boys. They had a terrible accident on Dug Road. Minutes after they left Christine off."

"A terrible accident?" Christine asked.

"The Cioffi boy was killed. The other one is in critical condition. They don't know if he'll make it. Linda's mother just called."

Mike? Dead? And Joe, maybe Joe, too? The twins looked in one another's eyes, took each other's hands. There was nothing to say. Mike? Dead? And Joe, maybe, too? Seventeen years old. Sixteen years old. Their friends? Dead?

"Linda's mother is so upset. She feels it's her fault. Letting Linda serve beer at the party. Well, it is in a way. Drunken driving.

Teenage drunken driving." Beatrice Baird's eyes blazed with anger and fear. "You're not to go in cars with boys again. Ever. Either of you. Do you understand me? Never. I'll pick you up myself."

The twins barely listened as she raved on. It was the same when one of their friends in grammar school got hit on her bike and was in the hospital with a concussion. Then she said they'd never ride bikes again. And of course within a week bike riding was back to normal. But this was different. Mike was dead. Joe on the critical list. And there had been drinking at the party.

Later, when their mom had calmed down, Christine said, "Mom, Joe drove me home. He wasn't drunk. He had maybe one beer all night and we were dancing it off."

Her mother finally let go of her and stood up. "You don't dance it off, young lady. And you don't drive my daughter home when you've been drinking. Period."

Christine had had it. "Mom, I know you're upset. But we're safe. Our friend Mike is dead, though, so could you please let up?"

The girls got dressed and went over to the drugstore to get the Sunday papers. A small crowd of kids was gathering in the little park behind the grocery store. Carolyn and Christine sat cross-legged on the grass and passed a styrofoam cup of coffee back and forth. By ten o'clock there were about twenty kids. Most of them were crying on and off, mostly on. And talking. About death. About life. About Mike.

Every once in a while someone would tell another story about a crazy, sweet thing that Mike had done. Like the time he found a litter of six kittens that had been left by the side of the road and brought them to school to give away. But first he gave each kitten a brightly colored punk-style "hair-do" with spray hair coloring. One had an aqua ear and tail. Another a bright pink streak down its back. They all found homes immediately and by the next day turned out to be pretty ordinary-looking kittens.

A state police car drove up. Was the trooper going to give them hell for hanging out, or something crazy like that? He strode over to them like John Wayne. "You kids friends of Mike Cioffi and Joe Trono?" he asked loudly.

They all mumbled, "Yeah," and nodded.

"I guess you know about Mike," he said. Would he be launching into the teenage drunk driving speech they had all heard at home that morning?

He put his hands on his hips and looked over the crowd. "I thought you'd like to know Trono's out of the woods," he said. Claps, cheers, and more tears. "I was just at the hospital," he continued. "Boy's got a bunch of broken bones and a messed-up jaw, but he's conscious now and he'll pull through." A couple of kids felt their own jaws. "I guess you all heard the accident was caused by drunken driving."

"Here it comes," Christine whispered to Carolyn.

"Well you heard right," the trooper continued. "But in all fairness you should know it wasn't your friend who was the drunken driver. There was another car, driving in the wrong lane from the opposite direction. He forced them off the road. Crashed himself, in Litchfield this morning. Doesn't have a scratch on him. We found paint from Trono's car in a fresh dent on his left fender. Trono confirmed it when he came to."

A few "Thanks for telling us" 's and a half-hearted cheer from the kids and the trooper was gone.

So was Mike. Forever.

Week Two

Chapter 3

"Help me, Nurse. Please help me." The weak voice, practically a whisper, was coming from Room 204.

Christine looked around, up and down the hospital corridor. No nurses.

"Please help."

Christine pushed the drug cart to the door and looked in. A tiny woman with short gray hair was trying to hoist herself up on her elbow. "I'm sorry to bother you," she said as Christine got closer. "The pain, nurse. It's so terrible." She tried to smile but it was defeated midway by a spasm of pain. "Is it time yet? For my next shot?"

Christine glanced at the name on the chart hanging on the footboard of her bed. "I'm sorry, Mrs. Stanley. But I'm not a nurse. I'll get one for you. Right away. Did you ring the bell?"

The woman nodded. "But remind them. Please."

She patted Mrs. Stanley reassuringly on

the arm. She was so frail, so desperate. "Of course. I'll make sure the nurse knows you need her." Then she rushed, cart first, toward the nurses' station at the center of the long corridor.

A dark-haired young woman, Lydia Johnson, was doing clerical work inside the square of counters. She looked up as Christine came to an abrupt halt with the cart.

"Well there's a speedy delivery for you," she said.

Christine knew she'd been going too fast. But she had a reason. "Listen. The lady in 204, Mrs. Stanley, is in awful pain. She's calling for a nurse."

The secretary looked at the panel of lights. The number "204" was blinking on and off. "I know," she said as she continued her work. "But is she dying? The woman in 201 is. Two of our nurses are in there with her. Or is she coming up from surgery? The boy in 219 is. And we'd better be ready for him. Mrs. Stanley," Miss Johnson continued, "is not due for her medication for another forty minutes." Then more sympathetically, "She'll have to wait."

"She's in an awful lot of pain."

Miss Johnson looked up at the clock. "Her husband will be here in a few minutes. Then he can harass us about her damn medication. Mrs. Stanley is a dear lady, but she does complain about pain. Low tolerance, I guess."

Christine moved the cart into its spot behind the counter. "The kid from surgery," she asked Miss Johnson. "Was that Joseph Trono?"

"Uh-huh. The kid in the accident over the weekend. You know him?"

Her heart pounded. Surgery?

"We go to school together. He's in my class." She didn't tell Miss Johnson that she'd been in the car minutes before the crash. "What was the surgery for?"

"I think they repaired some internal injuries and wired his jaw."

"Can I see him?"

"He's not up from recovery yet. It'll be a day or so before he's really with it anyway."

Christine looked down the hall, squinting at the little room number signs that extended above the doors. Rooms 202, 204, 208 on one side. Rooms 201 through 219 on the other side. Joe's room was at the far end of the hall. The opposite end of the floor from the elevator. Maybe she'd peek in on him tomorrow. See how he was doing.

She went toward the service elevator. As the doors opened, she backed away to give the orderlies room to move out a patient on a stretcher. IVs, a leg in traction, a wired jaw, glazed eyes filled with tears staring straight up at the ceiling. Joe!

Christine swallowed a little cry. On Saturday night, dancing legs and a big smile. Look at him now. She felt faint, took a deep breath.

He saw her. There was surprise in his eyes.

She put her hand on his arm. "Hi, Joe. It's

Christine. I work here, remember? I'll come see you tomorrow."

He tried to speak, but his jaw was wired shut. He looked back at the ceiling. Was he thinking what she was thinking? That she could have ended up on a stretcher, too, or in a coffin like Mike?

Christine couldn't get the pained and tortured look in those eyes out of her mind's eye all morning. When she got back to the pharmacy she did some more entries on the computer. But Joseph was there in her work, too, as she entered his medical data into the computer program. TRONO, JOSEPH. 3/16/85. DILAUDID 10MG. Q 4 H PRN. PHYSICIAN: DR. PISINELLI.

For lunch she got a tuna sandwich and an apple in the hospital cafeteria. She sat alone at a corner table. As she bit into the apple, she thought of Joe's jaw. Thompson, walking by her with his tray, stopped, and smiled down at her. "How's our intern doing? We working you too hard?"

Did he think she didn't like her work because she looked so glum? She smiled back at him as she swallowed her bite of apple.

"I love it. Working in the hospital. It's interesting. I don't know very much though. Like the other day with Dr. Pisinelli."

Thompson put his tray down and sat across from her. "Pisinelli's a special case. He's got a gruff way about him, but he's very particular about his patients. I wouldn't want to spend a social evening with him, but if I was going under the knife I'd be relieved to know Pisinelli was holding it."

Christine pulled some of the crust off her sandwich. "I have a friend in the hospital. Dr. Pisinelli operated on him this morning."

"Well, your friend is in good hands," Thompson said.

"They've put him on a lot of Dilaudid. What does that mean?"

Thompson took another big bite of meat loaf and swallowed it before saying, "Pharmacology 265. Dilaudid's a morphine derivative, and morphine — except for the addiction problems — is the perfect pain killer. It works in direct relationship to the amount of pain you're experiencing."

"I don't understand."

"Let me explain with the lab experiment we did in pharmacology lab. You take a rat and induce pain by giving it electric shocks. Then you give it a certain amount of morphine. If you increase the pain, you can increase the morphine dosage. If you decrease the pain, you decrease the morphine. But if you decrease the pain and increase the dosage of morphine, the rat has serious side effects. If you keep the morphine up and the pain down, the rat will eventually die. The only safe way to use morphine is in proportion to the pain."

"So if a patient is in a lot of pain they get more dilaudid?"

"Right."

"But it can be addictive?"

"Also right. You're a hip girl. You hear about heroin. Heroin's also a derivative of morphine."

"And people on heroin can overdose."

"Right again." Thompson had finished his meat loaf.

Christine had lost her appetite. She covered the rest of her sandwich with her napkin so she wouldn't have to look at it. Just the thought of those electric-shocked, squirming rats. Ugh.

Evenings at home were different for Christine now that Carolyn had homework every night and she didn't. Carolyn tried to get her work done before Christine got home, but there was always some left to do after supper.

"I'll do the dishes," Christine offered when they'd finished eating. "And you can work on your history paper."

"Nah. I'll help you with the dishes."

"And I'll help you with history."

"And I'll correct my papers," their mother chimed in as she pushed her chair away from the table. "By the way," she asked as she was leaving the kitchen. "When am I going to meet this Mr. Robert Connell?"

Carolyn and Christine exchanged a quick smile. "This weekend, Mom. He wants to meet you, too."

"Good," their mother said. "I like a young man with manners."

"Does he really?" Christine asked as they started the dishes.

"Does he really what? Have manners?"

"No, silly. Want to meet Mom?"

"I dunno. I thought it was a good public relations move."

"It was."

Christine filled the sink as Carolyn cleared the table. "You're so upset about Joe, Chris. Will you be able to see him tomorrow?"

She hadn't been talking about Joe with her sister, but then she didn't need to.

"Yeah. I'll go to his room during my lunch hour or when I get off for the day."

"You should wear the lab coat, though. Make it easier to get in. Some kids called the hospital from school and they said only his parents could see him."

She handed her twin a wet plate to dry. "Good thinking."

The phone rang. Carolyn put down the dish and dish towel. Christine's heart raced with her sister's as she said, "That must be Bob. He said he'd call."

"Carolyn," her mother called out. "It's for you. Robert."

He's not even my boyfriend, Christine thought. Why'd I get so excited?

She did the dishes alone.

The next day Gloria made the rounds with the drug cart while Christine transferred drug records to the computer program. For lunch she gulped down a yogurt, then she went up to the second floor. As she passed Mrs. Stanley's room she stopped and poked her head in. Mrs. Stanley lay there with her eyes closed. An elderly man — Mr. Stanley? — was reading to her from an old hardcover book. He stopped and looked up at Christine. "Is it time for her medication yet?" he asked Christine.

"I'm not a nurse," she said for the umpteenth time that week. "Sorry to bother you."

He squeezed his wife's hand. "Not yet, dear. In a little while. Try to concentrate on the story and breathe deeply. It will help." Mrs. Stanley opened her eyes. Her husband bent over and kissed her on the forehead. "My darling," he was saying to his wife as Christine left the room.

At the nurse's station Lydia Johnson was working on the charts, and a nurse was going over a patient's records with a social worker. Lydia looked up. "Hi, there."

"Hi. It's my lunch break. I thought I'd look in on Joseph Trono."

"Let me see." She went over to the medical charts and flipped through them. "Pisinelli's come and gone," she said. "He's just had his pain medication, so he's probably resting. I guess there's no harm in your popping in for a minute. But if he's sleeping, don't bother him."

Joe wasn't sleeping, or resting. He couldn't talk with his wired jaws. She knew he was in terrible pain. From the look in his eyes. From the sweat that streaked his black, curly hair. She felt silly, talking and not being talked back to. Just the pained stare of those dark brown eyes. It was hard to know what to say.

"Joe, everyone wants to know how you are. I'll tell them you're hanging in there. That it's tough but you're going to be alright." On and on for a couple of minutes that seemed more like a couple of hours. Then she said, "Mike's funeral's tomorrow. They had to wait for his older brother to get here from China. He was on some kind of tour. I'm so sad that you've lost your friend, that we've all lost him." Joe closed his eyes. Tears seeped out and fell on the pillow. She took his hand. He pulled it away and motioned for her to leave.

At the funeral the next morning she thought of those tears. Of Joe alone at the hospital while they were all able to share their grief. Why wouldn't he let her comfort him? Why did he motion her to go? Well, one thing was for sure: She was going back.

She went directly to work from the funeral. The drug carts had already been delivered and Gloria was making up drawers for new patients.

"How was it?" Gloria asked.

"Awful," Christine said.

"Sorry. That was a dumb question. I'm real sorry about your friend."

"Thanks. I think the best thing for me would be to keep busy. What should I work on?"

"It's been a quiet morning so I'm pretty well set here. Why don't you see if you can help Gary in the vault?"

She went to the locker to get her white coat. She could see Gary in the back of the vault. "Hi," she called as she was buttoning her jacket.

You'd have thought that she'd shot him in the back, he jumped so high. He turned toward her as she was coming into the vault. "God, you scared me." He was angry. "Knock first. Okay? This is pretty concentrated work."

"Sorry. I came to help."

"Well, I don't need any help." Was he swaying a little? He looked sort of pasty and pale.

"You sure?" There were little piles of drugs on the counter. It looked like there was a lot of work to do. She moved closer to the counter. "I'm a quick learner. Just show me what to do."

"I don't need any help. Just leave me alone." He seemed to want her to leave, like he was trying to think up something for her to do, to get rid of her. "The computer stuff I was doing this morning. You could finish that up. Go wait at my desk. I'll show you what to do in a minute."

He swayed. The blood drained out of his face.

"Gary, you alright? You look funny."

"I'm fine. Just go." He turned to the

counter. As she backed away he leaned on it for support.

She went back to the front of the pharmacy where Gloria was taking a coffee break. "Gloria, something's wrong with Gary. He looks awful."

"That's what I said this morning. But you know these macho guys. They don't let themselves get sick. His pride will keep him going. He probably partied all night."

Crash! A bottle fell to the floor of the vault. When they got there, Thompson was already out of his office and on the floor next to Gary. Hundreds of red and blue capsules rolled around the splinters of shattered glass.

"Smelling salts and water," Thompson ordered. Gloria went to get it.

Gary was coming to. "I'll be alright." He tried to sit up. "Just need some air."

"You're not alright," Thompson said as he felt Gary's forehead. "You've got a fever. It's this damn bug that's been going around."

Gary tried to stand. "Will you stay put?" Thompson said.

Gloria handed him the smelling salts and water.

"Get that stuff away from me," Gary said to the smelling salts. He drank the water.

"How'd you get to work this morning, big boy?" Thompson asked.

"Jack dropped me off. My car's being fixed."

"Good. We'll get someone to take you back.

I'd do it myself but I have a meeting with the nurses at eleven-thirty."

"I can take him," Christine offered. "I've got a car."

"And I'll clean this up and finish the control drugs during my lunch hour," Gloria said.

"I don't want to go home," Gary protested. "I'll be fine. Maybe if I had something to eat...."

"Give up, Gary. You're going home. We've got Chris to help out. If we have any questions we'll call you."

Gary sat next to Christine in the front seat of her mother's '76 Chrysler. He gave her directions to his house. "Take the road to Mount Riga for about three miles." They drove up into the mountain. It was a sparkling blue spring day. Early spring flowers were blooming along the side of the dirt road. Gary had opened the window on his side and was resting his head on his arm. The breeze blew his blond hair away from his face. Something's weird here, Christine thought. Why make such a big deal about leaving work when you're sick? It doesn't make any sense. And why wouldn't he let me help him with the control drugs?

"Penny for your thoughts," Gary said.

"Ah. I was thinking about how pretty it is up here," she said. "I'm glad it's finally spring."

Then she remembered Mike. And Joe in so much pain. On such a beautiful day. "What's wrong with your car?" she asked, just to make conversation.

"Sold it. I've got a new Trans Am coming in on Monday. Guy who bought my car needed it right away." He pointed out the window. "Make the next right."

She turned onto an even smaller, bumpier dirt road.

"The cabin is about half a mile down on the right."

"It's so out of the way," Christine said. "Real country."

"That's what I like. The peaceful life."

Was he joking around? He sure didn't seem like the kind of guy that went looking for peace and quiet.

The cabin was the only place on the road. A rustic-looking two-story place with a front porch.

"Is this yours? I mean do you own it?"

"Sure. Real estate is where it's at, you know."

She turned the motor off. He still looked terrible. "Do you want me to come in with you? Are you sure you'll be alright?"

He got out of the car. "I'll be fine. Just need some sleep." He put his head through the opened window. "Listen, thanks for bringing me home. I'm sorry about yelling at you before. Guess this bug was making me edgy."

"Forget it. Just feel better."

She waited until he'd gotten up the steps. He turned and waved good-bye.

Maybe he is the peace-and-quiet type, she thought. You never know about some people. You just never know.

With Gary out sick, Thursday and Friday were busy work days. Gloria delivered the drug carts while Christine did the computer entries. Then they both worked in the drug vault. During lunch and after work she visited Joe, checking in on Mrs. Stanley on the way.

Poor Mrs. Stanley always seemed to be in pain. "Dear, can you come here for a second?" she asked Christine during the Friday lunch hour. She showed her a get-well card her grandson had made and gave her a chocolate. And there was a fresh bouquet of daffodils to smell.

Joe's room was filled with flowers and cards, too. But nothing was taking the grief and pain out of his eyes. He didn't complain, even with gestures, but she saw it there. She'd brought a magic pad. He could write her notes, then erase them by pulling up the plastic sheet that covered the gray board. The nurse told her he'd have the wires on his mouth for at least two more weeks, but that he should be communicating. As she came into his room, she smiled but didn't say anything the way she usually did. She wrote on the pad and handed it to him.

Hi.
Let's talk this way from now on. Both of us. Do you feel any better today?

He read the note, then looked at his bed-stand. She saw the pencils and small pads. The nurses and his parents must have been trying to get him to write to them, too. He shook his head no.

She erased her first message with a rip of the plastic and wrote:

You're going to get better. You're better every day. Want me to bring you my Walkman and some good tapes?

He read it but didn't write an answer. She tried again.

What are you thinking about?

He looked at what she had written and picked up the pencil-like stylus. He wrote one word.

Mike.

She went to say something, but wrote in-stead:

I know. We're all thinking of him. But you've got to get better. You've got to think of positive things for that. What can I do to make you feel better?

He read it. Looked at her. Then wrote:

44

I would rather hear your voice than read your scribbles. Please talk.

She read it, didn't say a word, but wrote:

I'll talk if you'll write.

She pursed her lips sealed and looked him right in the eye. Had some life come back into them? He wrote back:

Deal.

"Alright!" she said, with a satisfied smile. The smile his eyes gave back was quickly darkened by a spasm of pain. He motioned her to go. It was time for her to be back in the pharmacy anyway. On the way out, she looked at the chart at the foot of his bed. He had had eight milligrams of Dilaudid half an hour before she came in. Why was he in so much pain?

Later that afternoon, Thompson stopped by Gary's desk where Christine was making entries into the computer. "How's it going?"

"Fine. But I have a question. Not about the computer stuff, about Dilaudid."

"I'm ready."

She swiveled the chair around to face him. "If someone has eight milligrams of Dilaudid every four hours, how would they be feeling?"

"Hmm. That's a heavy dosage. Well, there'd be periods of pain, say half an hour on either end of the medication."

"How would they be feeling half an hour after it was administered?"

"They'd be asleep. That's the time you doze off with that stuff."

"You sure?"

"Sure I'm sure. Drugs are my business, remember?"

She was embarrassed. And confused. Why was Joe in so much pain if he was having such heavy doses of Dilaudid?

Chapter 4

"You sure you want to do this?" Christine yelled to Carolyn.

Carolyn popped a soapy head out of the shower curtain and squinted at Christine. "Sure I'm sure. Now that we're going together he'll see how easy it is to tell us apart and everything will be all normal and nice."

"I'm not so sure," Christine said.

"I am," said Carolyn. But Christine knew she wasn't so sure either.

They'd agreed that they'd dress separately, in whatever they each chose. Since it wasn't Christine's date, she wasn't fussy. She threw on a pair of jeans and the light blue sweat shirt with the logo for the ice cream parlor she and Carolyn had worked in the summer before. LICKIN' GOOD, INC. the sweat shirt announced.

She went downstairs to talk to her mother while Carolyn got dressed. Beatrice Baird had insisted on setting out hors d'ouevres for "Carolyn's young man."

"Are you jealous?" she asked Christine as they were wrapping ham around cream cheese and long spikes of chives.

Christine put her arm around her mother's ample waist and gave her a squeeze. " 'Course not, Mom. Look how happy Carolyn is. Besides, after tonight he might not even be around."

"Well, all the fuss he's making about you being twins is silliness. If he really likes her so much he'll be able to tell the difference and he'll know it in his heart. Like, well, like I do."

"You've got a point. It's just — "

The doorbell rang. Ten minutes early. She looked out the dining room window. "There he is," Christine said. "I'll call Carolyn."

But Carolyn wasn't ready so Christine opened the door for Bob Connell.

He was very cute. Great athletic body, six feet tall, steel gray-blue eyes, and brown hair. A hunk in jeans and the black-and-gold Kennedy High athletic jacket.

"Hi," she said.

Before she could say, "I'm Chris," he looked both ways and said, "Where is she?"

"My mother? In the kitchen. She'll be right out."

"No. Your sister. I don't know, this is all so weird."

He was getting on Christine's nerves already. She put her hand on his arm. "Relax, will you? It's not such a big deal. You'll be able to tell us apart."

48

He looked in her eyes, leaned forward, and whispered, "I already can. I knew it was you right away." He planted a little kiss on her ear.

We are definitely getting off to a bad start here, Christine thought.

Carolyn came bounding down the stairs. "Bob, you're here — " she saw Bob with his arm around Christine " — early."

The girls just looked at one another. Carolyn's independently chosen outfit was jeans and a light blue sweat shirt advertising Lickin' Good, Inc. Bob took his arm from around Christine and went over to Carolyn with an extended hand. "Hi, Christine. Good to see you again." He looked from one girl to another. "I've got it straight. No prob."

Carolyn and Christine gave one another a silent signal. Carolyn shook his hand and said, "Good to see you, too, Bob." And to Christine she said, "Carolyn, let's go get some sodas."

When they came back into the room with drinks and the fancy hors d'oeuvres, Carolyn was Carolyn and Christine was Christine, and Christine had put her sweat shirt on inside out just so it would stay that way.

The plan was that they would all have what their mother called "a nice little visit." Then their mother would go off to the movies in Millerton with her friend Anita, while Christine went over to Linda's to hang out and watch tv. Carolyn and Bob could do what-

ever. It was pretty stiff and boring while
their mother was there. Mostly Bob was stiff
and boring, at least from Christine's point of
view.

At seven-thirty their mother said her good-
byes. "Shall I drop you off at Linda's?" she
asked Christine.

"Don't go yet," Bob said to Christine. "I'm
really beginning to feel the difference between you two." He smiled from one to the
other. "It'd help if you'd stay awhile. I've got
my dad's car. I can drop you at Linda's."

Actually, once their mother was gone and
they put some music on and Bob relaxed a
little, they had a pretty good time.

Christine told him some of her experiences
at the hospital, and about Joe.

"A group of us have been calling the hospital every day," Bob said. "They said it's
still too soon for visitors. Only the family."

"I think it would be good for him to see
kids from school," Christine admitted. Then,
thinking of Dr. Pisinelli, "But he has a strict
doctor." She thought of Joe, alone and in
pain, and wanted to be there with him, trying
to cheer him up. Making him feel better.

She tucked her legs under herself on the
couch. "So tell me everything that's going on
at school. The real dope."

"The real dope," Bob said, "is that there's
more dope going around school."

"Drugs dope?" Carolyn asked. "But that's
in any school."

"It was never this bad at Kennedy," Bob

said. "New stuff. Not just grass and cocaine, but lots of pills. Kids are popping all the time. To stay awake to study it's one pill, to sleep it's another, to play on the weekend something else."

"How come I don't know all this?" Carolyn asked.

"Because you're not in the boys' locker room. And you don't have friends that take drugs." He gave her another one of those little ear kisses.

Carolyn positively glowed.

Christine wanted to puke.

Well, Carolyn certainly doesn't have to worry about my being jealous, Christine thought.

But the stuff about the drugs was interesting. "Where does all this new stuff come from?"

"New York City, I guess. Maybe from the kids of the weekend people. Those kids are probably the dealers."

"Probably? Then you really don't know where they're coming from?"

"No one knows for sure. I'm just saying I figure the city kids are the dealers that get it here. Doesn't it all start in South America or someplace like that?"

"That's marijuana and cocaine," Christine explained. "Pills are another story. I expect they're all made in the good old U.S. of A."

Bob, his arm around Carolyn, said, "Maybe that's why they're all red, white, and blue."

"They are?" Christine asked.

"Just some red and blue sleeping pills I saw a guy buying in the john the other day. I guess they come in all colors."

"Yeah," Christine said. "They do."

In her mind's eye she saw the bottle shattered on the floor and the capsules rolling around Gary's prone body. Red and blue.

Week Three

Chapter 5

Monday morning Christine got to work early so she could check in on Joe before she went to the pharmacy. She had her Walkman to lend him and some of her favorite tapes.

As she got off the elevator on the second floor, she thought of Mrs. Stanley. She leaned into Room 204 but the bed was empty. Maybe she's down in X-ray, she thought.

"Hi, Joe!" She waved as she came into the room. He was sitting up in front of a breakfast tray of liquids. Anything he ate had to pass through a straw that could fit between the rubber bands that held his jaw shut tight. His eyes smiled at her.

"How was your weekend?" she asked as she handed him the magic pad from his nightstand. He wrote back:

Okay. How about you?

She told him about her sister and Bob and how he thought she was Carolyn. She told him what Bob had said about the drug scene at Kennedy, wondering if he knew more about it than she did. Then she gave him the Walkman and showed him the tapes she'd brought.

"I didn't know what your favorite groups were or anything, so I brought you my favorites. This is my number one." She held up the latest Bruce Springsteen tape. "I love the lyrics — they're so full of, I don't know, life . . . and hope. I figure that's what you need to get you through this."

Joe turned his head away.

"What? What is it?" she asked.

He wouldn't look at her. "Please. Tell me."

He turned back to her. His eyes were full of tears. He picked up the stylus and wrote on the magic pad:

That's Mike's favorite album. He knew all the words by heart. Would recite them over and over.

She slipped the tape in her pocket and put her hand on his. "I'm sorry."

They sat there, silently.

"Well, if it isn't the Florence Nightingale of Kennedy High," a voice behind her boomed.

Dr. Pisinelli! As far as Christine was concerned, Pisinelli was a perfect example of one of those doctors who think they're some kind of god. She took her hand off Joe's, stood up, and looked Pisinelli right in the eye. "Good morning, doctor. Joe and I go to school together. I just dropped in to say hello."

Pisinelli looked his patient over with his

trained eyes. "Doesn't look to me like you've cheered him up very much."

Joe had pulled the plastic to erase what he'd written on the magic pad. Now he wrote:

Chris is the best medicine I've had here.

He held it up for his doctor to read. "Oh, I see," Pisinelli commented as he took his patient's pulse. "Let's see what she's doing to your heart beat."

Christine blushed and looked at her watch. "Well, I better get down to the pharmacy. See you later, Joe."

Gary was back on the job after his illness. He still looked pale, but brushed off Thompson's suggestion that he take another day or two with, "Don't be silly. I'm fine."

Christine's first assignment of the day was to transfer drug orders into the computer. When she got to Orthopedics she looked Joe's order over carefully. The Dilaudid dosage was considerably less than it had been the week before. She wondered about Mrs. Stanley as she looked for her name in the records that she was working from. It wasn't there.

She went to Gloria at the picking station and said, "There's an entry missing in today's drug orders. Mrs. Stanley in Orthopedics."

"Lemme see." Gloria looked over the admissions/discharge sheet from the weekend, then up at Christine. "Stanley's a discharge."

"That's impossible. She was in terrible shape last week."

" 'Discharge' can mean 'dead,' dear. Mrs. Stanley died Sunday morning."

"She just had some broken bones," Christine protested. "How could she be dead?" That sweet lady, she thought. All that suffering.

"Here, check the admissions/discharge list for yourself. You'll be typing them into the computer later anyway." Christine looked down the list until she came to "Discharge. Mrs. Stanley, age 65. Respiratory failure." I don't get it, she thought. Something isn't right.

When Christine had finished her computer work, Thompson brought her into the drug vault where Gary was working. "She was good with the control drugs last week," he told Gary. "Let her give you a hand. That way you can leave early today. Get some more rest."

As soon as Thompson was back in his own office, Gary said, "Listen, I'm dying for a soda. Would you go get me one?"

She did.

After Gary had gulped down the soda, he said, "I forgot to get the paper this morning. Would you go upstairs and get one from the machine before they run out? I hate to ask you to do this stuff, but it'd be a big help." He looked at her with those tired, doe-like eyes. "Would you?" he asked.

She did.

Then it was, "Would you start transferring control drug inventory records into the computer? It'll save us time tomorrow."

By the end of the day she had spent about two minutes in the drug vault.

"Bob really likes you," Carolyn told Christine that night. "He says you're spunky."

Christine was sitting on her bed, painting her nails seashell-pink. Carolyn was at the desk working on her math.

"You know what would be perfect, Chris?"

"What?"

"If you had a boyfriend, too. It would be less complicated, don't you think?"

Christine wasn't paying much attention to Carolyn. She was thinking about Mrs. Stanley and Gary and ... the drugs at school. She felt they were all connected. Somehow.

Carolyn got up from the desk and sat cross-legged on the bed in front of her twin. "Chris." Christine looked up at her sister. "Something's bothering you," Carolyn said. "It has been all day. I knew it in school. I was so depressed I couldn't concentrate in my classes. I didn't even eat lunch."

"Me either."

"That's what I thought. It was you that was upset all day. What's wrong?"

Christine shrugged and looked down at her lap. "It's so complicated. I can hardly get it straight in my own head."

Carolyn put her hand on her sister's shoulder. "Look at me." Christine looked up. "For us, two heads are definitely better than one. Right?"

"Right."

"Double strength?"

"Double strength." Christine took a deep breath. "I'll tell you if you promise not to say I'm crazy."

"I promise. I just don't want us to be depressed tomorrow. Let's deal with it."

First Christine told Carolyn how weird it was that Gary minded leaving work when he was sick. Especially because he spent so much time at work trying to get out of working. Then about how much pain Mrs. Stanley and Joe had been in, when they were on high doses of Dilaudid. Then she took the leap over the big gap in her theory. "I think that Gary is stealing drugs from the patient supply at the hospital and selling them through dealers to kids at Kennedy."

"Chris, that's crazy."

Christine screamed, "You promised."

Carolyn cringed. "Sorry. Let's take it from the top again."

They went over it all again.

"But why?" Carolyn asked. "Why would he do it? Where's the motive?"

"Money. You saw the yearbook. His ambition is to make a billion. You don't do that on an assistant pharmacist's salary."

"Come on. Everyone says silly things in a yearbook."

"C., he just bought a new sports car. He owns his own house. And he wears this T-shirt that says, 'The guy with the most things in the end, wins.'"

"Maybe the guy's got a rich uncle."

"Maybe he sells drugs to kids," Christine answered.

"Even if he does, you need more evidence than a new car, a cabin in the woods, and a T-shirt!"

"Agreed. So let's figure out how we can get some."

They put their minds together and thought. They focused on the problems silently, in unison. That's how they got through physics. Maybe it would work now.

After a few minutes they looked up at one another, smiled, and simultaneously said, "That's it!"

"All we need," Carolyn said, "is the opportunity for you to mark the pills."

"And," Christine added, "someone to place an order at school."

Later, when they'd been in bed for an hour, Carolyn rolled over and faced Christine. "I can't fall asleep. Something else is on your mind. You haven't told me everything. It isn't depressing, it's some kind of question. Please tell me. I — we — need our sleep."

"It's Joe Trono, C. I think I really like him."

Carolyn sat up and turned the light on. "Chris, that's terrific. But why aren't we sleeping? Are you worried about his legs?"

"Partly. His left leg's pretty bad. But that's not what's keeping me awake right now. What I wonder is, do I like him out of sympathy or do I really like him."

"You mean, like, are you just feeling connected because you can help him and it makes you feel good."

"Yeah."

"I guess we can't do anything but wait and see how you feel about him when he's better."

"And stay awake wondering," Christine said.

"And stay awake wondering," Carolyn sighed.

Chapter 6

Sunday, Christine was assigned to work at the hospital with Gloria. There'd be just the two of them, which was why it seemed like a perfect time for Christine to make her move.

"You better duck," she told Carolyn as they pulled into the hospital parking lot. Carolyn scrunched up in a ball on the floor of the car.

As Christine got out of the car she checked her watch. "See you in five minutes," she whispered through the window to her twin.

When she got off the elevator at the basement level, she walked past the pharmacy to the service entrance. As she was looking up and down the corridor to see if the way was clear, the janitor turned the corner with a box of garbage for the dumpster. He'd be going out the door where Carolyn was waiting to be let in.

"Mornin'," he said as he went toward the door.

"Good morning," Christine answered. "I'm

going out back for some air. Why don't I take that for you?"

She extended her arms.

"Don't mind if you do," he answered as he handed her the box.

The janitor continued on his way.

Christine opened the door.

Carolyn slipped in.

Now what? If only they could merge their bodies the way they did their minds, Christine thought.

"I'll go into the pharmacy and find an excuse to get Gloria into the back office," she told Carolyn. "You hide in the second partitioned office on your left. Stay there until she leaves with a drug cart."

Half an hour later Christine and Gloria had finished the first two drug carts. Gloria said, "See, working on Sunday isn't so bad. You take Orthopedics and I'll take Pediatrics. We'll be back here in no time."

"Fine," said Christine.

"Let's go, then."

"Ah . . . Gloria, can I ask a favor?"

"Sure, you can always ask."

"I . . . I had a fight with my boyfriend last night. I feel awful about it. I'd like to call him. Privately. Would you mind going ahead? I'll get out with my carts in five minutes. I want to make up with him before it's too late. I was so bitchy."

Gloria put a sympathetic hand on Christine's shoulder. "Some favor. Of course you can. Call your guy. There's plenty of time to do the carts. I'm relieved you don't have a crush on break-their-hearts-and-run Sanders." She studied Christine. "You don't, do you?"

"No way," Christine said. But remembering those steel-gray eyes, she couldn't help wondering. Do I?

As soon as Gloria was gone, Carolyn came out from Gary's office. "This is crazy," Carolyn whispered. "I feel like a sneak. I don't know, Chris. Maybe we should just stop all this right now."

Christine held her twin's hand. "Come on, Carolyn. I'm counting on you."

Carolyn let out a resigned sigh. "Get me a jacket."

At the lockers Christine pulled out the other medium lab coat and handed it to Carolyn. "Do you remember what to do?"

"Sure I do. But I'm real scared. What if we get caught?" She looked at the drug vault. "If you get caught."

Christine felt for the eyebrow tweezers and plastic baggie of yellow confetti in her pocket as she looked at the drug vault. She was scared, too, and Carolyn knew it.

As Carolyn was pushing the drug cart into the hall, Christine called her back into the pharmacy. "You need this," she said as she took off her name tag.

Carolyn pinned the name "Christine Baird" to the lapel of the lab coat. While waiting for the elevator, she reviewed in her head the floor plan her sister had taught her.

Meanwhile Christine went into the drug vault to put miniscule nicks in a hundred white Dilaudid tablets, and to add the tiniest piece of yellow confetti to the contents of a hundred red-and-blue Tuinal capsules.

Carolyn was getting through the drug cart delivery like a pro. When a staff member addressed her by name, all she had to do was smile, read their name tag, and return the salutation.

At the nurses' station she was greeted by Dr. Pisinelli. "Well, how's Florence Nightingale today?"

"Fine, thank you, Doctor." She read the tag. So this was the famous Dr. Pisinelli.

As she was pushing the cart into the corner, Pisinelli watched her. "It's a wonder you get any work done. All the time you spend romancing my patients," he said gruffly. "By the way, Mr. Trono said if I saw you to ask you to stop by his room."

She looked over the numbers and names on the drawers. Room 219. Trono, Joseph. "I . . . sure . . . I'll stop by."

Carolyn left the cart and headed down the corridor. "Miss Baird," Pisinelli bellowed. "You're going the wrong way."

She looked down the corridor. No Room 219. "Silly me," she said to Pisinelli as she turned on her heel and went the other way.

Carolyn didn't want to have to play a twin game on Joe. Fooling the staff so that Christine could do her detective business was one thing. Fooling Joe was something else.

"Ah, hi," she said as she walked into the room.

Joe was tubed up, wired up, and in traction. She walked over to the bed and smiled down at him. A chill passed over her. This could have been Christine in a hospital bed, she thought. Or worse, she could have been in the coffin that they watched being lowered into the grave on Monday. How could she have lived without her twin? Impossible.

"I can only stay a minute," she told Joe. "Gloria and I are alone in the pharmacy today." He looked disappointed. "You're looking better today."

Joe picked up the magic pad and wrote:

When I'm better will you go out with me?

Carolyn was struck dumb. What would Chris want her to say? Or do? Chris, I hope I'm not messing you up here, she thought as she smiled down at Joe and said, "Sure. That'd be fun. Ah . . . we can double date with my sister and her boyfriend."

Joe's face clouded over. He studied her for a second, erased the pad, and began writing again. Did he know she wasn't Chris? She picked up the pad and read:

I'd rather be just us. Two of you that look alike is too confusing. One's enough for me.

"Okay," Carolyn said. She smiled again. "But I've got to go now."

What did Chris do when she left? Just say good-bye? Or kiss him? To be safe Carolyn bent over and kissed him on the cheek. "Take care, Joe. Really."

Joe held on to her arm to keep her from going. Then he wrote:

Bring back Mike's music. Okay?

What did he mean? Mike's music. Mike was dead. Maybe Chris would know.

"Alright. I will," she said. "Tomorrow."

He lay back on the pillow. There was so much going on in his eyes. But Carolyn didn't understand any of it. Would Christine? she wondered.

"So how did your call to your boyfriend go?" Gloria asked her when she got back to the pharmacy.

Remembering Christine's excuse to get Gloria to leave the pharmacy first, Carolyn said, "Good. I'm glad I called. I feel better. We made up." She smiled at Gloria. Chris was right. Gloria wore the most amazing shade of eye shadow. "Thanks again."

"What'd I do? Nothing," Gloria said. "So you want to go to lunch first?"

"No," Carolyn said a little too emphatically. "You go first." She rubbed her stomach where armies of nervousness were at war. "I had a big breakfast. I'm not even hungry yet."

Gloria left for the cafeteria.

Carolyn went to the back of the pharmacy and knocked on the vault door.

Christine opened it.

Carolyn handed her the name tag. There wasn't time to talk about Joe now. "Gloria just went to lunch."

"Good," Christine said. "I'm almost finished here. You better go."

And Carolyn very gladly left the way she came.

When she got off the hospital grounds, she walked the half mile into town to meet Bob at the drugstore at twelve sharp, as planned. Bob didn't know it yet, but he was part of Christine's scheme.

They bought sandwiches and chips for a picnic at the lakefront. It was a warm spring day. More like May than early April. She figured she'd wait until he'd had a good lunch and was nice and relaxed before she asked him.

When they'd finished eating he lay back on the blanket and looked at the sky. "You know, Carolyn, no two clouds are alike. No two snowflakes are alike. No two leaves are alike." He pulled her toward him for a kiss and hug. "And you know what?"

"What?"

"I don't believe any two people are alike either." He stroked her hair. "I've decided there's no such thing as identical twins. You and your sister may look a lot alike but you're very different. You just have to be encouraged to go your separate ways."

Carolyn decided not to argue the point. Besides, the moment had come to ask Bob to do his part in Christine's plot. First she gave him all the background stuff that Chris had explained to her. Then she told him where he figured in.

He sat up. "What do you mean, 'other drugs'? That's crazy. It's dangerous."

"It's an adventure. And we might just figure out how all that stuff is getting into school." God, Carolyn thought, I sound just like Chris.

"But why should we get involved? If it's her idea, let her follow it through. I don't want any part of it. People who mess with the drug trade end up in the bottom of rivers wearing cement shoes."

Maybe he's right, Carolyn thought. Why am I getting involved? But she knew why. "Chris'd do it for me if I asked her. And all you have to do is put in an order for Dilaudid tablets and some Tuinal capsules. Chris wrote down the street names for them." She held out an envelope. "There's twenty dollars in here, too. You give us the pills. Kids get drugs every day at school. You won't be in any great danger."

He looked at the envelope in her hand. "You really want me to do this, don't you?"

"Yeah. I do."

He took the envelope. "Then I will."

"Great."

"But understand one thing and make sure

Chris does, too. I'm not doing it for her. I'm doing it for you."

Carolyn was thinking, What you do for one of us you do for both of us. But that didn't seem like the sort of thing she should tell Bob.

Week Four

Chapter 7

Christine had to be at school by one o'clock. The kids in the career seminar who were out on jobs were required to come in for one afternoon midway through their six-week work stint. There'd be a general discussion with the students who were doing classwork, about what it was like to work in the "real world." Then after school they'd have individual sessions with the teacher, Mr. Rubins.

Christine was headed for the second floor when someone tweaked her rear. She turned around to swipe the guy across the face. Her arm froze in midswing. Bob Connell.

He ducked. "Carolyn, it's just me."

"I'm Chris," she said as she dropped her arm by her side.

His face fell. "I thought I knew the difference."

"Geez, Bob," Christine said impatiently. "Don't get so upset. Lots of people look alike from behind." She couldn't resist adding, "especially identical twins."

He looked at her resentfully. "Well I sure can tell the difference face on." Then he told her that the only reason he was cooperating with her "harebrain" scheme was because of Carolyn. That yes, he'd placed the order for "Mr. M" and "Candy." And as soon as he got the drugs on Wednesday, he'd turn them over to her — as fast as he could.

"Who'd you order them from?" Christine asked.

"Some zonked out kid from my math class who was hanging out in the john. He'll give the order to someone who gets them from someone else."

"Oh. I wish you'd found out where they came from. Couldn't you probe a little?"

He leaned forward and whispered angrily, "You can't ask that sort of thing. People'd get suspicious." He nervously checked his watch. "I better get back to class."

She headed for the stairs as he looked cautiously both ways before heading down the hall.

"Bob," she called after him.

He turned. "Yeah?"

"Thanks. I appreciate it."

"You're welcome, I guess."

"And Bob."

"Yeah?"

"I really don't think you need the sunglasses."

* * *

Christine couldn't wait to get to work on Tuesday. There was something that she wanted to ask Thompson. As soon as she'd said good morning to Gloria and Gary, she put on her lab coat and went to Thompson's office. The door was open. He looked up from his desk. "Morning, Christine. What's up?"

"I have another question."

He indicated the chair. "Have a seat."

She closed the door behind her and sat at the chair across from her boss. "Remember you explained about the rats and the morphine?" she began. "I, ah, have to write a report for my career seminar, about what I'm learning. I want to include that stuff about the rats and morphine, but there's something I don't understand."

He leaned back in his swivel chair and tapped the pencil eraser on his desk. "Glad to help. What's the question?"

"If a rat was in great pain, you know, from high voltage shocks, but was on very little or no morphine, and you suddenly increased the morphine to the level that it should be for that amount of pain, what would happen to the rat? I mean, being that the dosage is suddenly appropriate to the pain."

"If the morphine level was suddenly raised, even though the pain had been intense, it would be too much too soon. The rat would show adverse effects. It might even kill it. An overdose."

"Could that even happen in hospitals?" she asked.

He sat up. "Could what happen?"

"That a patient wasn't getting the dosage you thought he or she was getting, so they . . . overdose?"

"It could happen, but it doesn't. That's why we have so much accountability over the control drugs."

"I see," Christine said.

Thompson looked over the pile of papers in front of him. "Any other questions?"

"No," Christine said as she stood up to leave.

She did have another question. But it would have to wait until she could ask it of the right source — the computer. That opportunity didn't come until lunchtime when Gloria and Gary were off to their separate lunches and Thompson had closed his office door, saying he didn't want to be disturbed.

Christine went to the computer and inserted the disc with Mrs. Stanley's medication profile. She scrolled until she came to the prescription drug orders.

She had a theory that she wanted to test out. First she looked over the dosages of Dilaudid for the last two weeks of Mrs. Stanley's life. What if, she asked herself, the Dilaudid dosage Mrs. Stanley was getting wasn't full strength? What if her doctor and nurses thought she was getting eight milligrams, but she was actually only getting four milligrams? Christine changed the entries.

Wherever there were eight milligrams of Dilaudid prescribed, she entered four milligrams.

Then, she wondered, what if on the last night of her life she got the prescribed full dosage? She checked the last entry. Sixteen milligrams of Dilaudid! Pisinelli must have upped her prescription when he saw she was experiencing intense pain on what he thought were eight-milligram dosages. She left the last dosage at sixteen.

What she was asking the computer was, if Mrs. Stanley was only getting four-milligram dosages of Dilaudid, and then suddenly received a sixteen-milligram dosage, what would happen? She typed in the formula for checking out the acceptability of Mrs. Stanley's prescription and hit RETURN.

The computer whirred.

The screen flickered its green-on-black response. WARNING. OVERDOSE. COULD BE FATAL.

Christine stared at it. If someone was stealing Dilaudid from the patients to sell on the street, and then wasn't around to steal it any longer, it was possible that the patient could unwittingly be given an overdose.

"So, Florence Nightingale, where's your boss?"

Christine was catapulted from her thoughts by Dr. Pisinelli's stern voice. As he leaned over her shoulder to see what was on the monitor, she turned it off.

"So, you're a computer whiz, too. Why'd

you turn it off? Not because of me, I hope."

Did he see the screen? How long had he been standing behind her? She swiveled around to face him. With ultimate cool she said, "I just finished what I was doing, Dr. Pisinelli. If you're looking for Mr. Thompson, he's in his office. But he said something about not wanting to be disturbed."

"Good," Pisinelli said as he headed for Thompson's office and opened the door without knocking. "Thompson," he boomed. "I got a question and you're the only one in this fool place who'll know the answer. You'd think this whole institution was being run by high school kids, the slipshod way things are handled around here." He closed the door behind him with a bang.

Christine leaned back in the chair and thought. Warning. Overdose. Could be fatal. How did Mrs. Stanley die? She couldn't risk asking the computer with Pisinelli in the other room and Gary and Gloria due back from lunch break any minute. The physician's orders for medication for Mrs. Stanley from last week were in Gary's bottom drawer. She took them out and flipped through the pile until she found, 'Stanley, Bertha.' Scanning the record she came to the last line. 'Patient died. Respiratory failure.'

"I'm back. You can go to lunch now," Gloria called from the front of the pharmacy. Christine put the file back in the bottom drawer and picked her pocketbook up off the floor. Gloria was coming toward her, eating the last of a chocolate ice-cream bar.

"I'm ready for a break," Christine said as she stood up and stretched.

"The chicken's pretty good today. Nice and crispy."

"I brought a sandwich. I'm going up to Orthopedics to visit my friend Joe. You know, from the accident."

"I thought you had a boyfriend," Gloria said.

"No, that's — " She almost said, "That's my sister," then remembered how she'd told Gloria on Sunday that she needed to call her boyfriend. "I mean, Joe's just a friend." She dashed out of the pharmacy. "See ya."

Because of the school meeting on Monday, and Carolyn visiting Joe in her place on Sunday, and no work on Saturday, Christine hadn't seen Joe since Friday. And in the meantime Carolyn had said she'd go out with him and kissed him good-bye. Well, truth was Christine would love to go out with Joe and truth was she couldn't wait to see him. As she got off the elevator, thoughts of seeing Joe, of his speedy recovery, of their dating pushed aside her theory about drugs going from the hospital to the high school, of Mrs. Stanley's death. Joe had had three days to get stronger. Maybe they've loosened the rubber bands in his mouth so he can finally talk, she thought.

Christine bounced into his room with a

big smile that turned into a gasp. "Oh, my God," she said in a shocked whisper.

Joe's left leg was back in traction, his mouth was still shut tight with metal bars and rubber bands, and he was moaning in a painful, fitful sleep. Intravenous solutions were dripping into his body.

She tiptoed to the foot of his bed and picked up the chart. "3/15 Surgery." They'd operated yesterday. Tears filled her eyes. Why did he have to suffer so? Why hadn't anyone told her?

She moved up to his bedside table, picked up the magic pad and wrote:

Came by for a visit, but you were asleep. Was at school yesterday. Didn't know about the operation. Will come back tomorrow.

Chris

She propped it against the lamp where he'd see it when he woke up. She picked it up again to add the word "Love," above her name. Well, she thought, that's what I feel. I guess.

On her way out she stopped by the nurses' station. Mrs. David was distributing pills into individual paper souffle cups for the next round of patient medications. One pill in here, three in there, two in there.

"Mrs. David," Christine interrupted. "Joe Trono was operated on yesterday. What'd they do to him?"

"X-rays showed a floating chip near the

break so they did some emergency repair work. Apparently it wasn't mending right anyway."

"Is it serious? I mean, will he be able to walk alright?"

Mrs. David went back to her medications. "You'll have to ask Dr. Pisinelli," she said. Christine knew that if Mrs. David was sure that Joe would be alright, she would have said so.

At the end of the day, Christine and Thompson were the last to leave the pharmacy. As they were walking to the elevator she said, "For this report I'm doing, when I'm discussing the rats and morphine. . . ."

"Those little buggers again," Thompson chuckled.

She pretended a casual laugh. "Yeah. The rats. What I wonder is, when they overdose, on morphine, what happens? I mean, how do they die?"

"Why, respiratory failure. Morphine's a central nervous system depressant. It depresses the respiratory regulatory center in the brain. The rat stops breathing."

"Oh," Christine answered. "Respiratory failure. . . ." She finished the sentence in her head. ". . . just like Mrs. Stanley."

As Christine was driving home, she reviewed the evidence. If the pills that Bob got today are the ones that I marked, well then I'll know they come from the hospital. So then what? Will I go to the police with the evidence? Tell Thompson?

Up to this point, figuring out a "mystery" had been sort of fun. Even exciting. Playing the twin switch at the hospital. Marking the pills. Getting Bob to place the drug order. Now it felt like an enormous burden. There was such an imperative to figure it all out — as fast as possible. Because now she was convinced that there were lives at stake. If Mrs. Stanley had died of an overdose of morphine, then other patients on morphine, particularly in Orthopedics, like Joe, were in danger. She remembered him tossing in pain. Was he receiving the correct dosage of Dilaudid? Or was the medication he needed being sold to his classmates at Kennedy High?

Bob's motorcycle was parked in front of her house. Christine tried to be casual when she gave her mother a kiss on the cheek. "Hi, Mom. Where's C.?"

"In the backyard with Robert," her mother answered. "Such a nice young man," she muttered to herself as Christine dashed out to the yard.

Carolyn and Bob were in a clinch of a hug. Good grief, Christine thought. Mom should see this "nice young man" right now. All he wants is to get in my sister's pants.

She cleared her throat, "Ah, hi, guys. You got the stuff?"

Bob looked up at her without taking his arm from around Carolyn.

"Hi, C.," Carolyn said.

As far as Christine was concerned, Carolyn looked absolutely, ridiculously silly. I hope I don't look that silly when I'm so-called "in love," she thought.

Bob picked up a small Burger King bag with his free hand. "Your little mystery ends in that bag," he said. "Let's just hope this nonsense hasn't gotten any of us in trouble."

Carolyn shrugged herself free of Bob.

"What do you mean?" Christine asked.

"I — we — opened some of the capsules," Bob said. "No little yellow pieces of paper, Sherlock Holmes. I told you all the drugs come from New York." He held out the bag. "Take a look for yourself."

She grabbed it. "Just because it isn't in some doesn't mean it isn't in the others. And that doesn't account for the Dilaudid." She put the paper bag in her pocketbook and started toward the house. "I'm going in."

Carolyn looked from Bob to her twin. "Me, too," she said as she gave Bob a quick peck on the cheek. "Chris, wait," she called as she ran after her sister.

Carolyn locked their door and Christine took out the Burger King bag. First she opened the baggie of white tablets and laid them out on the green desk blotter. Then she took the spy glass from the drawer and studied the tablets one by one.

Carolyn sat on the edge of the bed, watching her. "I'm sorry," she said. "He's being a jerk. He's not like that when I'm alone with him."

Christine didn't answer.

"Chris, talk to me."

Christine turned and looked at her sister.

"No nicks in the pills, huh?" Carolyn said.

"No nicks."

"Well, I guess that's it," Carolyn sighed. "I'm sorry about the way Bob acted. I really am."

"Don't worry about it. I don't care."

A knock on their door. Christine brushed the pills into the baggie.

Carolyn went to the door and opened it. Her mother was standing there. "Dears, that nice young man is leaving. He said he would call you later, Carolyn." They all listened as Bob's motorcycle revved up.

"Thanks, Mom," Carolyn said.

"Is everything alright?"

"Everything's fine, Mom."

Beatrice Baird patted her daughter on the shoulder. "Ah, young love can be so complicated," she said. "I'll be in my bedroom if you need me."

Carolyn closed the door. She sat on the edge of the bed again and watched as Christine opened the capsules, one after another. Christine stared at the pile of powder and the red and blue capsule shells. Not a smidgen of yellow confetti.

"*We* haven't given up," Christine answered. She sat next to her sister on the bed.

"Carolyn, Gary could have stockpiled drugs. He just may not have gotten to the stuff I marked when he filled Bob's order."

"That's possible," Carolyn agreed. "So?"

She silently connected with her twin's thoughts.

"Oh, no," Carolyn said as she jumped up. "No. No. No. I just can't ask him to do it again."

"He's calling later. Let me talk to him. I'll just say I'm you. I can convince him."

"No way. No more twin switches on Bob. Do you understand?"

"Then you're not going to help me figure this thing out?"

There was a long pause.

"I'll do it," Carolyn said. "I'll ask him myself."

Christine gave her sister a hug. "Thanks."

Why is it, Carolyn wondered, that when I'm with Chris everything that we're doing makes perfect sense. That it feels like what we have to do. But when I'm with Bob it seems like silly, dangerous nonsense?

Bob called at eight o'clock. On the dot.

When Carolyn explained that they wanted him to put in another order for drugs, he said he wanted to talk to Christine.

"I'm not doing it, Chris," he said.

"We need you," she told him. "If you won't do it, Carolyn will. But the trouble with that," Christine continued, "is someone might think she's me. I mean the whole thing that we're twins and I work with the main suspect makes it pretty dangerous for her. Don't you think?"

"Carolyn shouldn't do it either."

"It's Carolyn or you."

"Don't you have any other friends?" he asked.

"We shouldn't let anyone else in on what we're doing. It compounds the risk of being found out. And at this point we've bought drugs. We can't prove that we did it for a worthy cause." She paused. There was silence on the other end. "Will you do it?" she asked.

"I'll do it. But know this, Christine Baird. If Carolyn had gone on the first internship and you were the one I went out with, we wouldn't have gotten past the first date. Just know that. I'm definitely going out with the right twin."

Yeah, Christine thought as she handed the phone back to Carolyn. But I'm not so sure my twin is going out with the right guy.

Saturday was Christine's day off, but she went to the hospital anyway — for two reasons. The first was to visit Joe.

"Hey, Florence," Pisinelli called as she passed the nurses' station. "Your boyfriend has a surprise for you."

She wouldn't let herself smile at him, but she did say, "Thanks."

As she continued toward Room 219, Pisinelli said to the nurse, "It's not visiting hours yet. Are we letting these high school kids come in here anytime they want just because they're volunteers?"

"I don't think she's a volunteer," the nurse said. "She works in the pharmacy."

Christine swung into Joe's room. "Hi, Joe," she said as she approached his bed.

He handed her the magic pad. He'd already written something on it:

I can talk.

She looked at his mouth. No rubber bands. No metal bars. "You can talk? That's wonderful," she said. "So talk."

He shook his head.

"Come on."

He pursed his lips.

"Why are you giving me such a hard time?"

He smiled, but still he shook his head no.

"Does it hurt to talk?"

He shook his head again.

She looked him over. One leg in traction, the other leg in a cast, and an IV in one arm.

"I'm going to tickle you if you don't talk," she said.

He didn't say a word. His eyes were laughing.

She leaned over him, her hands closing in on his torso. Just as her finger tips were about to start the tickle-torture she had in mind, he grabbed her left hand with his free one, and said the first words she'd heard from him since the night of the accident.

"I like you, Christine," he said softly. "A lot."

Now Christine was the one who was speechless.

"I like you, too," she finally said. "A lot."

They talked for an hour. First about little stuff. He told her how boring it was to be a patient and she told him all the gossip from school. They made plans about the things they'd do when he got out of the hospital.

"I may have a limp," he said. "I don't know if I'll be able to dance or play sports that much."

"I don't care," Christine said. "I mean, I care for your sake, but it doesn't make any difference in our going out or anything. Besides, you might be alright."

He suddenly looked downcast. "I hope I do."

"Hope you do what?"

"Have a limp."

She couldn't believe what she was hearing. "Why?"

"As a punishment. For killing Mike." He looked her straight in the eye. "So I'll never forget."

"Joe, that's crazy. You didn't kill Mike. It wasn't your fault." Could it be he didn't know? "My God, didn't they tell you? There was another driver. A drunk, driving in the wrong lane."

"I know. But Chris, I was kidding around with Mike when I was driving. Not paying a whole lot of attention to the road. If I'd been more alert, I know I could've gotten us out of the way in time."

What could she say?

"All of this." He gestured to his legs, the IV, his mouth. "All of this pain is only a drop in the bucket compared to what I deserve."

"Joe," Christine cried, "that's wrong. That kind of thinking is wrong, all wrong. Accidents happen. How do you know what would have made a difference? How can anyone know that?"

"I've been thinking about it a lot. I know."

The nurse came in to check his pulse and temperature. She touched his face gently. "Listen, Romeo. I'd go easy on the talking if I were you." She nodded to Christine as she took his pulse. "He needs to rest."

Christine leaned over and kissed him on the cheek. "I'll come back tomorrow." Then she whispered in his ear, "You've got to stop thinking like that. You're wrong. I was in the car with you, too. I know."

She looked him in the eyes once more before leaving. She'd learned to read his eyes and she knew that he didn't believe her.

The second reason she'd come to the hospital on her day off was to pay a surprise visit to Gary Sanders.

"Anybody home?" she called out when she came into the pharmacy.

"Be right there," Gary called back from the depths of the vault.

He came to the front of the pharmacy only after closing both the day gate and the vault door. "Well, hi there," he said to Christine. "What're you doing here? If you want Gloria, she's in the cafeteria."

"I just stopped by to say hi," she said with her most direct smile. "To you."

He was surprised. "You did?"

"Uh-huh. I was visiting a friend and thought I'd see how you're doing down here."

"Oh, I see."

She sat on the edge of Gloria's desk. "I've been thinking. You and I work together almost every day, but we never get to — I don't know — really visit."

He studied her. "And you'd like that?"

"Yeah. I'd like to get to know you better, Gary Sanders."

"I thought you had a guy. That kid that was in the accident."

She had to swallow hard and look anywhere but in Gary's eyes when she said, "Joe's a friend from school. I visit him because we're friends. But he's not my boyfriend."

"Oh, I see."

"So I was wondering if maybe you'd like to, I don't know, go out some time." Christine had never, ever been this forward with a guy. She couldn't believe that she was doing it now.

Gary looked her over — top to bottom and back up again. "Yeah. I'd like to go out sometime. Maybe next weekend? I've got a party to go to on Saturday. How about Sunday night?"

"Sure," she agreed. "Sunday night."

"So," he said.

"So," she said. "That's settled. Sunday night. But I'll see you this week. Here."

"Right," he said. "Of course."

He put his hand out and touched her cheek. "You're real pretty, Christine Baird. Real pretty."

When she was back out in the hall she gritted her teeth and shook herself. She had the heebie-jeebie creeps just from being with him. And she'd just made a date with him! The worst part was that the date wasn't for herself. It was for Carolyn!

And the worst, worst part was that Carolyn didn't even know about it.

I won't tell her just yet, Christine decided.

Week Five

Chapter 8

Christine was lying on her bed looking at the ceiling. She'd taken the first shower. "I guess I really do like Joe, separate from the sympathy stuff."

Carolyn was brushing her hair out in front of the mirror. "It sure sounds that way," Carolyn agreed. "And feels that way."

Christine rolled over and hoisted herself on her elbow. "Do you like it?"

"Like what?"

Christine sat up. "See. You said, 'Like what?'" Three weeks ago you would have known what I meant without asking. Do you like being separate the way we've been? Me on a job, you at school, you with Bob, me maybe with Joe."

Carolyn turned toward Christine. "I don't think of us as separate. It's like we're together even when we're not."

Christine got up to stand beside Carolyn in front of the mirror. They looked at each other, wet hair falling to their shoulders.

"I still think of us as one. Don't you?" Carolyn asked.

Christine nodded. "Yeah, I do. I just wonder if we always will. I mean with different men and jobs and then kids of our own someday. I just wonder."

They looked in the mirror again. Both remembering when they'd played house as little kids. Pretending that they were married to identical twin men — two of Johnny Simpson from their third-grade class to be exact. That they lived in identical houses connected by an enclosed walkway. And that they had babies at the same time, babies so much alike that they could have made up a set of identical twins.

"It'll never be like it was when we played house, though," Christine said.

"I know," Carolyn answered.

Bob's motorcycle *put-putted* up the block. "The drugs," Carolyn said. "He must have picked them up after school."

Christine headed for the door. "Let's go."

"No. You stay here. I'll go. It's better if you don't see him today."

Well, thank God there aren't two of Bob Connell, Christine thought as she sat at her desk.

Carolyn was back in a couple of minutes. "Here," she said breathlessly as she handed Christine the Burger King bag. "I better talk to Bob for a bit. So Mom won't think it's weird that he came and went so fast."

Christine took the bag. "Carolyn," Christine said before she sat down to inspect the drugs. "Tell Bob thanks. By the way, we don't look alike anymore."

Carolyn's face lost its glow. She ran her hand over her wet hair. "What do you mean?"

"You have a big hickey on your neck; I don't."

Carolyn ran to the mirror. "Oh my God. Mom'll see it."

Christine took a red bandanna from the scarf rack in their closet and handed it to her. "This should take care of it."

With Carolyn gone, Christine sat down at the desk and took the two baggies of pills out of the paper bag. She just stared at them as her heart pounded its way to her throat. If these pills aren't marked, she thought, I'm giving up. I'll accept I'm wrong, break the date with Gary, and accept that Mrs. Stanley's death was inevitable. If they're marked, I'll know I'm right — at least about them coming from the hospital pharmacy. And what I wish, she finally realized, is that they aren't marked and I can get on with my life. Because I don't like having my heart pounding in my mouth.

She swallowed hard and laid the five Dilaudid tablets out on the blotter. Then she took the spy glass out of the middle desk drawer and turned on the desk light.

She peered down through the magnifying glass at the first pill. To the right, above the dividing mark across the center of the pill, there was a tiny nick.

Her breath quickened. Calm down, she instructed herself. It could be a coincidence. A nick that got here from bouncing against other pills. She looked at another. The same nick. And the third, the fourth, and the fifth. All with nicks, right where she'd put them.

Her palms started to sweat as she took the first of the ten capsules out of the bag and opened it. No yellow confetti.

She opened another, and another, and another. No confetti. He must have a big stockpile of Tuinal, she thought.

The door to her room burst open. "It's just me," Carolyn said, as she closed the door behind her. "They're the pills you marked, aren't they?"

Christine nodded.

"I knew it," Carolyn said. "I knew when I was downstairs, just the way I'll always know." She looked her twin in the eye. "Even when we're apart."

The motorcycle pulled away from the house. "So, C.," Carolyn said as she sat on the edge of the desk and looked down at the pills. "What do we do now?"

Christine looked up at her. "There are a lot of unanswered questions, aren't there?"

"There sure are." Carolyn picked up a red capsule. "And there's a capsule you haven't checked."

Christine opened it and turned out the

contents. On the top of the tiny pile of granules sat a piece of yellow confetti.

The next afternoon, Gloria asked Christine to deliver the control drugs to the floors. "How far ahead are they on these pills?" Christine asked.

"What do you mean?"

"Well, like the drugs that Gary counted out today and that I'm delivering, when will they be used? Right away?"

"Oh no. The stock is kept at about a four-day level."

"So the pills I'm delivering now won't be used for four days?"

"Roughly, that's right." Gloria looked over Christine's shoulder. "What's up, Gary? You couldn't be looking for something to do for a change?"

"Don't sweat it, Gloria. I'm just eavesdropping."

Christine didn't turn around. Gary had heard her asking about the drugs that she suspected he'd been stealing. Did he know she was suspicious of him?

She did some calendar work on her fingers as she waited for the elevator. Gary got sick on Wednesday, April 9th. Mrs. Stanley died on Sunday, April 13th. One, two, three, four. Four days later. Four days later when she might have been given the prescribed dosage of dilaudid that was really an overdose.

The elevator came. Two nurses moved to

the back to make room for the cart. But, Christine thought, wouldn't the medical staff notice that there were medications missing? Did Gary have a partner on the floor who administered incomplete dosages of drugs to their patients?

She rolled the cart off the elevator and over to the nurses' station on the cancer floor. Every pill of every control drug that came into the hospital had to be accounted for. And loads of nurses and all of the pharmacists were involved in that accounting. They couldn't all be willing to let patients suffer needlessly in order to sell drugs on the street. But if drugs were missing, why hadn't someone else figured it out? She knew drugs were missing — at least five Dilaudid pills and ten Tuinal capsules had not been administered to patients. They'd been sold to Bob. The numbers weren't working.

Later when she was making entries on the computer, Gary came over and bent down, supposedly to look at the monitor over her shoulder.

He whispered in her ear, "I've been watching you all week. I'm looking forward to Sunday night."

Keep your cool, Christine warned herself as she turned and smiled up at Gary. "I'm looking forward to it, too."

When he was back in the vault, she sat there staring at the monitor. What did he expect of her on Sunday? Had she gone too far in flirting with him? Especially since she was substituting her twin for herself on the date.

"Substituting," she whispered to the monitor. Of course. That's it. He's substituting some other kind of pills for the control drugs. That way the numbers work. If he takes five Dilaudid tablets, he puts in five of something that looks like Dilaudid. Sugar pills, or aspirin, something nonprescription that he can easily get. Then the nurses don't even know. And the patients don't know. They just suffer.

Like Joe.

Like Mrs. Stanley.

Like how many other patients?

It was five o'clock. "Want a ride home?" Gary asked, as he walked by the desk.

She pretended she was looking for something in her purse, so she wouldn't have to look at him. She was afraid he'd see the suspicion and fear on her face. "Oh, no. I have my mother's car. Thanks anyway."

He rubbed the back of her head. "Well, here's to Sunday night. See ya."

"Sexy," he mumbled to himself as he walked off. "That girl is definitely sexy."

Their mother had parent/teacher's night at her school so the twins were making their own supper. A super-salad supper. The big glass bowl already had lettuce, fresh asparagus, tomatoes, and spinach.

They'd gone over Christine's plan for Sunday night and Carolyn had readily agreed to be Gary's date. "As long as I don't have to ask Bob to do anything else," she said.

Christine looked in the back of the refrigerator. "Hey, here's a chicken leg from Sunday. That'll be good."

She cut up the chicken and a hunk of feta cheese while Carolyn made a dressing.

"C., I think the date with Gary is a mistake," she told Carolyn. "Maybe I should just take the evidence I have to the police or something."

"You need more than that. You know we do. The date is a good idea."

"I can't put you in a car with that guy. He's dangerous — in more ways than one. He probably has ten hands — all looking for my ass, which on Sunday night will be your ass. Maybe I should just search his cabin on Saturday night. He said he's going to a party."

"Chris, what you're doing is much more dangerous than what I'm doing. Now stop worrying and take the baggie you just cut up out of the salad."

Chapter 9

"So what'd you tell Bob?" Christine asked, as the twins were getting dressed for their "date" with Gary Sanders on Sunday night.

"That you and I haven't gone out alone in a long time. So we're going to the movies."

Christine tossed Carolyn a red crewneck sweater identical to the one she'd just put on. "What'd he say?"

" 'That's nice.' Something like that."

"Come on, C. What'd he really say?"

Carolyn's head poked through the neck of her sweater. "That it probably was a good idea. Maybe then you wouldn't be so jealous of him."

"Jealous? Of him?" Christine brushed her hair with angry, hard strokes. "He can't possibly think I'd want to go out with him."

"Not jealous of him that way." Carolyn wasn't looking at Christine as she put on her boots. "He says you're jealous of me, meaning I'm not with you when I'm with him."

"Oh," Christine said matter-of-factly as

she sat on her own bed and pulled on her own boots. "That goes without saying."

They looked up at one another. "And," Carolyn went on, "he thinks you've gotten involved in this whole thing with the drugs at school and everything as a way to keep me in your life. That it's all a reaction to the separation, and to him."

They thought about that. Finally Christine said, "Bob just might be smarter than I thought he was."

Beatrice Baird was already in her bathrobe and curled up on the couch in front of the tv when the girls came downstairs. They each kissed her good-bye.

"Wait a second," she said without looking away from the tv. "Here's a commercial." While two tv housewives rhapsodized about the best toilet bowl cleaner, their mom told her twins, "Have a good time. I like seeing you go out like this, together. Seems to me it's been a long time. You know, over the next few years boys will come and boys will go, but you'll always have each other."

"Yes, Mom. And we have you," Carolyn said.

"But I'm not waiting up for you tonight. If you don't mind."

"Fine, Mom. Fine," Christine said, a little too enthusiastically. "Get to bed early."

She smiled at her girls. "In by eleven?"

"Yup."

"I feel so much safer when you're together. I know you watch out for each other."

A wave of guilt went through Christine's body.

But their mother didn't notice. The commercial was over and Carolyn and Christine were on their way to the garage. The second they closed the car doors and were ready to roll, nervous energy took over.

"Okay," Christine said as she backed the car out. "Let's review it. You're meeting him outside Four Brother's Pizza. I'll leave you off two blocks away."

"If he says anything about my walking, I'll say that I was baby-sitting nearby."

"Right. And C., don't let him get out of taking you to a movie. At least there'll be other people there."

"And if I can, inspect his glove compartment, in case he's stashing stuff there."

"But be careful."

"Chris, you be careful. Ah, you don't think this character is going to know I'm not you? I mean, look how Bob can tell now."

"Don't worry. I'm not tuned into him at all. He won't know." She pulled up to the curb. "Besides, I'm not so sure we couldn't fool Bob."

Carolyn's face dropped.

"I mean if we had to, needed to. But not like for intimate stuff."

"Chris."

"Uh-huh."

"I hope we couldn't."

They exchanged a final glance. "Go to it," Christine said. "Just be sure he brings you home right after the movie. I'll be there."

"What if Mom's up? She'll wonder where I am."

"I'll tell her you bumped into Bob. That you'll be home in a half-hour. Just be sure to do whatever you have to do to get rid of him after the movie. I don't care if he hates me. He will anyway when we blow this thing open. And C., under no circumstances should you end up in that wilderness place of his."

Carolyn got out of the car. "Got it."

"See you at home in a few hours."

Gary was spiffy clean and looking very cute when Carolyn met up with him a few minutes later in front of the pizza place. Not bad, she thought. If I wasn't going out with Bob, and this guy wasn't probably a drug dealer, I could see where Chris could really fall for him.

"So, Christine Baird, nice to see you on off hours." He looked her up and down. "You look just as good at night as you do during the day. Maybe even better."

"Thanks," she answered offhandedly. "So do you." She checked her watch. "Gee, we better hurry if we're going to be on time for the movie."

He held up a video tape. "I got the tape of *Yellow Submarine*. Thought it might be fun to bring it back to the cabin and watch it on my VCR." She felt a moment of panic.

"We can get a pizza, lay back. No hassles. Promise. We won't do anything you don't want."

"What I want," Carolyn said a bit peevishly, "is to go to the movie theater and see *Splash*. Like we planned."

"They're both underwater," he tried.

God, she thought, if I'm too bitchy he'll just call it off and go home. She smiled at him. "*Splash* is supposed to be very good and I've seen *Yellow Submarine* a thousand times. Truth is, I'm a little shy; I mean, seeing you like this. I'd really rather start by going to a movie."

Gary put his arm around her shoulder. "Baby, I'm convinced." He threw the cassette in the backseat of his car through the open window. "Let's go."

As they stood in line for tickets Carolyn said, "My purse. I left it in the car."

"It'll be okay," Gary said. "I locked the doors."

"I need it."

"No you don't. I'm paying, baby. None of this women's lib stuff."

"No. I mean I need it for something else. My . . . you know."

Even Gary Sanders could blush. "Yeah. I see. Want me to get it?"

"Why don't you get the tickets and popcorn? Popcorn'd be great. I'll be right back."

She looked over the keys as she crossed the street to Gary's black Trans Am. Two big ones, two small ones. So the key to the glove compartment must be on this ring, she thought. She unlocked the passenger door. Her purse was on the floor where she'd intentionally left it. Across the street she could see Gary buying their tickets in the brightly lit lobby of the small theater. Unlocking the glove compartment, she kept one eye on him. She riffled through maps, a notepad. No drugs. She put everything back and closed the glove compartment. She picked up her purse and went to the movies with Gary-ten-hands-Sanders.

I wish I'd known I'd be coming back here, Christine thought as she drove up Mount Riga. I'd have paid better attention to where that turn was. It was a dark, moonless night. That was a disadvantage, too. She left the high beams on and drove slowly. Were there three mailboxes at the first turn? Or four? She tried to remember. She drove past a clump of three boxes, and when the next turn had only one, she turned around and went back. She made a left. What if I go into the wrong place? she thought. And get caught! About half a mile down the road she took a right and bumped along the dirt road until her lights picked out the cabin. She went beyond the cabin and parked in a stand of trees.

With a flashlight, extra batteries, gloves, and a racing heart, she made her way through the field to the cabin. The front porch light shown brightly and alone in the dark night.

She circled the house to the back door. The door was locked. She tried the kitchen window. Unlocked. She raised it, climbed on a wooden bench, and came into Gary's cabin via the kitchen sink. Better remember to move that bench back to the yard, she reminded herself. She unlocked the kitchen door to insure making a more graceful and, if necessary, speedy exit.

The flashlight would have to do for light. Dozens of carpenter ants scurried from the beam of the flashlight that led her search through the kitchen cupboard. She explored every opened container. Cornflakes, sugar, flour. Box after box, jar after jar. No drugs. Then the refrigerator. Old bread, yogurt, milk. Not even a container worth exploring in there.

His bedroom, she thought. Flashlight first, she went through the living room and up the stairs. A door to the right, one to the left. She tried the left one. Her flashlight beam did a quick once-over. Double bed, bureau, pile of dirty clothes, closet. Where to begin? As she sat on the bed to think for a second, she let out a little yelp. She was sinking, wobbling, floating. A water bed.

Jumping up, she said to herself, I'm finishing this search and getting out of here. First, the bureau drawers. Lots of underwear, unmatched socks, crinkled shirts, old baseball cards, a high pile of ten- and twenty-dollar bills tucked in a corner — but no drugs.

A car screeched to a halt in the driveway. She froze. What was he doing coming back so early? Was Carolyn with him? She silently shut the drawers as the front door opened and closed.

A man's voice. "I can't wait for you. I just can't wait. Come on."

A woman's voice. "Where's Gary?"

"Getting himself another virgin. I have fifty bucks saying he won't score the first night."

"Can we use his waterbed?"

"Fine with me. As long as you're in it."

They were coming up the stairs.

Christine opened the closet door, sat on the floor, tucked her knees under her chin, and closed the door.

She heard the bedroom door open and close. The man and woman fell on the waterbed, cooing and giggling.

Who were they?

When would they leave?

How would she get out?

Carolyn had trouble concentrating on the movie. Whenever she'd begin to get caught up in the story, she'd start worrying about Christine at the cabin, or wondering how she was going to get away from Gary after the movie.

She was also preoccupied keeping Gary

from getting too far with his touchy-feely stuff. Finally the movie ended. The lights came on. As they walked up the aisle toward the exit, Gary leaned against her from behind and whispered in her ear, "Now let's go to my place and make this romance a double feature."

She turned to face him. "I . . . ah . . . have to use the facilities. Meet you in the lobby."

"Right."

She dialed home on the pay phone between the GALS door and the GUYS door.

After the third ring her mother answered. "Hello."

Carolyn put a tissue over the mouthpiece to disguise her voice. "Hello. Is Christine there?"

"Well, no. The twins went to the movies. Would you like to leave a message?"

"No. Thanks. I'll call tomorrow."

Christine wasn't back. What had gone wrong? Was she still at Gary's cabin?

Carolyn was hanging up the phone when Gary came down the stairs. "Hi, there. Who were you talking to?"

"Ah . . . my mother." She gave him a sly smile. "To tell her I'll be a little later than I thought."

"Alright, baby. We're on our way."

The road up Mount Riga was pitch dark and isolated. What if they met Christine in the car, going away from the cabin? Would Gary recognize it?

"What you doin' way over there?" he

108

asked. His hand reached over and stroked her leg. "You're awful quiet." He turned and smiled at her. "You don't have to be afraid of me, you know. You heard Thompson. I'm harmless."

They turned into his drive. "There's a car," she said. She put her hand over her mouth. Had she shrieked it?

"I want to be alone with you, too, baby. It's just the guy I share the house with. We have our own rooms. Not to worry."

"No. I mean. I didn't know you . . . uh . . . had a roommate. That's all." Where was Chris? Had the roommate found her? A shudder passed through Carolyn. "I'd like to meet him," she said.

They came in the front door. There weren't any lights on. Gary flicked on a table lamp. "Where is he?" Carolyn asked. "Your roommate."

Gary put his arm around her. "You're shaking, baby. Calm down. Jack's probably in his bedroom with some broad. Come on. I'll give you the grand tour — and we'll skip his room."

He led the way. Carolyn followed, focusing her mind totally on her twin. Where are you? she thought over and over.

"Here's the kitchen."

She looked around the bare but cozy room. "It's nice." He was closing the window. "I thought I closed that," Gary said. "Funny."

That's how she came in, Carolyn thought. So she's here. Or she left in a hurry.

She followed Gary out of the kitchen. He took her hand. "Sweaty palms, baby. Really. Calm down. I never would have taken you to be so shy. You're really gutsy at work." He led her back into the living room and toward the stairs. "Just come with me. I'll show you the rest of the palace." She followed him. As she climbed the stairs she began to feel Christine's presence.

"And what's upstairs?" she said loudly so Chris would hear them coming. Gary threw open the door at the top of the stairs. "This," he announced with a flourish, "is my room."

Carolyn gave out a shriek of surprise as the startled couple on the waterbed pulled the sheet over them. Gary shouted, *"My* room, with my goddam roommate using my bed!"

The guy and Gary guffawed. The girl wasn't even embarrassed. Neither was Carolyn, really. She was just frightened. Frightened for Christine because she knew she was hiding in the closet. How can I get everyone out of this room? Carolyn wondered.

"Jack Curtis, Sally McCormick, this is Christine Baird. Christine, this is Jack and Sally."

"Hi," Carolyn said. "Nice to meet you." She turned to Gary. "I feel cold. Do you think we could have a fire?"

"Sure. A fire. Think I could have my room back, Curtis?"

"We're finished with it," Curtis grinned as

he threw his legs over the edge of the bed and drew on his jeans.

As the four of them left the room, Carolyn made sure she was the last to leave. She closed the door behind her.

Christine raised herself out of the cramped position and cautiously, quietly, opened the closet door. What now? How would she leave? And how would Carolyn get away from Gary?

As she was coming out of the closet to stretch and think, her foot knocked against a backpack. Glass clinked against glass inside it. She turned on the closet light and closed herself in again. She bent over the bag and unzipped it. Bottles filled with tablets and capsules. She opened a bottle of white tablets and took one out. She felt gently around the edges, then held it up to the light, peering intently at the circumference. The nick was there. Three out of the next six pills she inspected had the same marking.

Jack and Sally were making popcorn in the kitchen. Carolyn sat on the couch watching Gary stack wood in the fireplace. "They'll be gone in a little while," Gary assured her. "Jack and I respect one another's privacy, if you know what I mean."

Carolyn stood up. "I'm going to the bathroom. Be right back."

When she was halfway up the stairs he

reminded her, "Hey, there's one down here."

She leaned over the rail. "Silly me. I forgot. Well, I'm halfway there. Be back in a jif."

Christine heard the steps, the voice. She closed the bottle and the bag, and was standing in the middle of Gary's bedroom when Carolyn opened the door. They let out a big sigh and silently went into the bathroom. As Carolyn turned the water on, their voices overlapped excitedly.

"God, I was so scared."

"What a mess."

"I've got to get you out of here."

"*You've* got to get out of here."

"We've both got to get out of here. And, Carolyn, I found the pills I marked. They were in the closet."

They both calmed down. They weren't nervously excited anymore. They were quietly terrified.

"C., what are we going to do?" Carolyn asked.

Christine unclipped her hair and shook it loose. She took Carolyn's pocketbook, found her comb, and brushed her hair in the style identical to her twin's.

"What are you doing?" Carolyn asked.

"I'm going downstairs to finish off this date."

"No."

"Yes. I know him better than you do. I can handle him. I'll distract him. You just get out of here."

Carolyn put her hand on Christine's arm. "I don't want to leave you."

"Please. You go. I know I can get myself away from him."

Carolyn let out a resigned sigh. "How do I get out?"

"Through the kitchen door. I unlocked it."

"His roommate and that girl are in there."

"Then we'll have to play it by ear. Listen for your chance."

They heard the bedroom door open. "You okay in there?" Gary called.

"Coming," Christine answered.

Carolyn flushed the toilet. "The car," she whispered in her sister's ear. "Where is it?"

"Clump of trees to the right a few hundred feet up the road. You'll see it."

"Be careful," they whispered in unison.

The toilet flush was still. Christine put her sister's bag over her shoulder and pointed to the bathtub. Carolyn got in and lay down as Christine silently pulled the curtain closed.

"My turn," Gary told Christine as she came out of the bathroom. He put his arm around her. "Why don't you just wait for me here, take a little ride on my waterbed."

"I'll meet you downstairs," she said as she pulled away. "But hurry."

Carolyn lay in the cold porcelain tub listening to the sound of the toilet flush as Gary said to himself, "Well, Sanders, looks like you got yourself a good time and fifty bucks to boot."

* * *

Gary and Christine met Jack and Sally at the bottom of the stairs.

"We're going up to Jack's room." Sally extended the bowl of popcorn. "Want some?"

"No thanks," Christine said.

Gary took a big handful.

"Great fire," Christine told Gary as they sat on the couch.

He put his arm around her and pulled her closer. She didn't resist, but cuddled up to his embrace. "How about some music?" she suggested.

"Okay." He got up and looked through a pile of tapes next to the stereo. "Here's something quiet and romantic."

"I'd rather listen to something loud and sexy," she told him. Loud enough so Carolyn can sneak down the stairs and out of here, she thought.

"Now you're talking, baby."

He put in a Rolling Stones tape and turned up the volume. "You know," he said as he sat close to her again, "you're like a different girl from the one who went upstairs a few minutes ago. I think I like this one better."

There were kisses and hugs and lots of touching. "I like to go slow," Christine whispered in his ear.

"Me, too," he mumbled through a wet kiss on her ear.

She overcame her repulsion and fear by concentrating on Carolyn. Now, she thought as hard as she could. Now is the time to come down the stairs. Hurry.

Christine kissed Gary on the eyes, all over his face, then a passionate one on the lips. When they broke off the kiss to catch their breath, she knew her sister was safely out of the cabin.

She also knew with the most horrible, sinking feeling that she had both sets of car keys — Carolyn's in the pocketbook, her own in her jeans pocket. And they were at least eight miles from home, up a dark country road.

Did Carolyn even know the way?

"Let's go upstairs," Gary whispered in her ear.

She pulled away. Straightened up. "It's late, Gary. I have to go home."

"What? Now? We're just warming up here."

He grabbed for her.

She stood up. "No. I really should be getting home. I . . . I mean it's only our first date. I'm sorry if I led you on."

"Playing sweet little high school girl, huh?" He put out his arms. "Come on. What we had going there was very good. Let's not ruin it."

A door upstairs banged shut. Hadn't Carolyn gotten out after all?

Footsteps on the stairs.

"Christ," Gary muttered. "More interruptions."

"Don't let me bother you," Sally told them as she reached the bottom step. "I'm going home. Music's too loud and your friend up there has a lousy bed."

Christine jumped up. "Do you live in town? Can I get a lift?"

Sally grinned maliciously at Gary. "Sure. Why not?"

Gary cursed. "Is that creep Jack splitting the bet with you?" he asked Sally.

"What bet?" Christine asked.

"Nothing," Gary told her. "Some little thing between me and my corrupt roommate."

"I'd appreciate the ride," she told Sally. She kissed Gary on the cheek. "Thanks for the movie. See you tomorrow."

She picked up Carolyn's purse and followed Sally to her car.

As they drove down the mountain, Christine kept her eyes peeled through the darkness for Carolyn. Would she know enough to duck into the bushes if she heard a car? Or would she try hitching a ride? What would Sally think if they stopped to pick up Christine's identical twin on this deserted road?

They made it to town without spotting Carolyn. But now Christine was afraid Carolyn had lost her way on one of the side roads.

She asked to be dropped off in front of the drug store. "It's my corner," she told Sally. "I can walk the rest of the way. I'm late so I want to sort of sneak in."

"I can dig that," Sally said. "See 'ya."

"Good-night," Christine told her as she got out of the car. "And thanks."

As soon as the car had turned the corner, Christine went into the phone booth in front of Landon's Pharmacy to call Bob Connell.

He answered the phone. "Hello?"

"Bob, it's Chris. I'm in front of the drug-store. Can you come over on your motor-cycle? Right away."

"Why? What's going on? Where's Caro-lyn?"

"There was a mixup with our car keys. She's with the car on Mount Riga, but she doesn't have her keys."

"Mount Riga? I thought you went to the movies. What's going on? What have you done? I'm not getting involved in this drug thing any more than I am. Do you know that the kid in my math class is giving me free samples because I'm such a good cus-tomer? Just keep me out of this."

"Are you going to let Carolyn walk eight miles down Mount Riga in the middle of the night?"

Silence. Then, "Where are you?"

"In front of the drugstore."

He slammed the receiver down and was there in three minutes. He barely looked at her when he braked his cycle in front of the drugstore. "Get on," he ordered as he handed her the rider's helmet.

The cycle screeched away from the curb and sped through town. As they passed the post office a state trooper suddenly pulled out, drove past them, and cut them off.

"Damn," Bob muttered to her as he pulled over and turned off the engine. They both got off and faced the trooper.

"License," he demanded.

Bob opened his wallet and handed over his license.

"Give me the wallet, too," the trooper said. "And turn your pockets inside out."

"What? Maybe I was going too fast, sir. That's no reason to search me."

"Who said anything about a search, Sonny? Just turn your pockets inside out."

"But . . ." Bob protested.

Please, God, Christine prayed. Please, God, don't let him have any drugs on him.

Bob turned his pockets inside out. The three of them watched a small cellophane bag of white powder fall to the ground.

"Someone gave it to me," Bob protested as the trooper bent to pick it up. "I didn't even want it."

"Sure," the trooper agreed. "You tell us all about it at the station. Seems to me if someone is giving you free samples, you must be a valued customer."

He turned to Christine. "You, too, young lady. Empty your pockets and give me your purse."

Her car keys fell to the ground. He rummaged through the bag and inspected the wallet. He looked up at her. "So, Miss Carolyn Baird, what are you doing on a motorcycle with a druggie at eleven o'clock on a Sunday night?"

"What?" Bob looked over the trooper's arm at the opened wallet. "You said you were Christine."

"I am!" Christine cried. "It's Carolyn's purse. Her identification. I can explain."

"So who are you?" the officer asked.

"I'm Christine Baird. It's my sister's pocketbook. I borrowed it."

The trooper turned to Bob. "Buddy, you don't even know who you're out with? We're giving you a blood test."

"I can explain," Christine said. "Carolyn and I are twins. Identical twins. And officer, it was my fault. I gave him that, ah, stuff."

"No she didn't."

"Yes I did."

"Hold it!" the officer boomed.

"You, Miss Baird, get in the car. I'm dropping you off at home. You," he said, pointing to Bob. "Get on that cycle and follow me." He held up Bob's wallet before sticking it in his uniform jacket pocket. "And no funny business."

No one had ever looked at Christine with such fury and hatred as Bob Connell did just then. The worst part of the glare was the hurt in it. Because at the moment Bob didn't know if he was angry at Christine or hurt by Carolyn.

As soon as the cycle and cruiser were out of sight, Christine walked back through town and started the lonely, dark walk up Mount Riga. I was right, she thought. Gary's been stealing drugs from the pharmacy and selling them to the kids at school. But look what's happening. My sister's walking down Mount

Riga, probably lost. And her boyfriend's at the police station being booked for possession of cocaine. What now? What on earth do I do now?

Take one step at a time, Christine, she answered herself. One step after another, up Mount Riga to find Carolyn and get the car. That's a start.

An hour later she saw a shadow jump into the woods. Carolyn, she thought real hard. It's me.

Carolyn came out and ran toward her sister. They hugged.

"Thank God you're alright."

"Thank God you found me. I didn't even know if I was on the right road."

They were both crying.

"Where's the car?" Carolyn asked.

"It's still in the woods near Gary's."

"Oh, no!" Carolyn moaned as she turned around and faced the stretch of mountain she'd just come down.

They retraced Carolyn's steps up Mount Riga. The only energy they had was from a roll of tropical fruit Lifesavers that Christine found in the bottom of Carolyn's purse.

When they'd gone about a mile, Carolyn turned to her twin. "What is it? What are you keeping from me?" she asked.

"Nothing. I told you I found the marked pills in the closet, that Gary's really the thief."

"That's not it, C. There's something else.

You're trying not to think about it so I won't pick it up. There's something you're hiding from me."

Christine gave up. There was no way to keep a secret from Carolyn. "It's Bob," she admitted.

"What happened? You didn't call him or anything? He doesn't know what we did tonight?"

"It's worse than that. He's in jail."

"What? Why?"

When Christine finished her explanation, Carolyn screamed at her twin. "You did this! You got him in trouble! He'll have a criminal record now. You've ruined his reputation, probably his life. Bob's right. You're messing up everybody's life."

"But I was right about the drugs, Carolyn. That's what's important. I can straighten out this whole thing with Bob and the police tomorrow. I promise."

"What about tonight? Why didn't you do it tonight?"

"It's gotten too complicated. I mean it's not like we went to the police. They found us, with drugs. They wouldn't have believed me. They wouldn't have searched Gary's place on my word. Not yet. You've got to trust me."

"Trust you? That's what I've been doing and look at us."

Christine looked around them. They were halfway up Mount Riga. A bolt of lightning and a clap of thunder marked their first fight.

Rain poured on them for the next hour. Finally they reached the car. They drove home in silence.

That night, for the first time in sixteen years, the twins went to bed without wishing each other sweet dreams and a good night's sleep.

Week Six

Chapter 10

"Hey, my sleepy people, get up and cheer," Jay Towers boomed from the innards of the clock radio.

Christine moaned as she switched it off and reached for her covers. They were on the floor and she was curled up in a chilly ball at the top of her bed. She'd snuggled her whole body into her pillows. As memories of the night before emerged from her sleepiness, tears welled up in her eyes. "Oh, C.," she begged out loud, "please don't be mad at me. I feel so lost without you. Please."

Silence.

Christine straightened out her aching, cold body, and looked over to the other twin bed.

Empty.

"Carolyn!" she screamed. Where was she? Christine ran into the bathroom. Empty.

The bedroom door opened and her mother came in.

"Are you alright?" her mother asked. "I heard you call for Carolyn."

Her mother went over to her. She put a hand on each of her daughter's arms.

"Where is she?" Christine asked.

"Didn't she tell you? She had to be at school early, some kind of meeting. You both look so tired. I shouldn't have let you go out on a Sunday night. You don't look well, Christine. Are you sick?"

Christine pulled herself up and tried to smile reassuringly at her mother. "I'm alright, Mom. I just forgot that Carolyn had to be at school. I got frightened when I didn't see her."

Her mother shook her head sympathetically and patted her daughter's arm. "You're so close. Always have been. I guess you always will be."

I wonder, Christine thought as she went into the bathroom to shower. I wonder if we always will be.

I wish I'd confided in Joe, she thought on the drive into work. Maybe I wouldn't feel so lost and awful. And there's no time to explain now. Maybe if I can see him for a few minutes. Make contact. It'll give me the strength to get through this day. When she got to the hospital, she took the elevator to Orthopedics on the second floor instead of to the pharmacy in the basement.

Joe looked weak, but gave her a big smile anyway. "Hi. How you doing? I didn't expect you until lunchtime."

She bent over and kissed him on the lips. A nice long kiss like they'd never done before.

He reached up and stroked her hair. Being with Joe like this wiped away the kissing and touching with Gary from the night before. They looked into each other's eyes. Silently, but full of understanding. Like when she looked at Carolyn.

"What's wrong?" Joe asked. "What is it?"

"Nothing," she started to lie. Then she corrected herself. "I had a fight with Carolyn. It's the first time. I . . . it's awful. I have to make up with her."

"What'd you fight about?"

"It's complicated. I'll tell you later. I have to get downstairs." She looked at his left leg, hung above them in the traction. "Tell me about you. How's your leg?"

"They took X-rays. Later today I'll know whether I'll walk straight or crooked."

She trembled. "Today?" She squeezed his hand. "You'll know today?"

"Yup."

"Oh, God." She bent over to kiss him goodbye. "I'll be back later."

"Christine," he whispered in her ear. "I'm scared. I do want to walk straight again. For you."

She looked at him, intently. "What about yourself?" she asked.

His eyes told her that he wasn't ready to forgive himself for the accident. Not yet.

"Morning," Gloria sang out when Christine came into the pharmacy. "As soon as you're ready, could you bring the control drug stock to the floors?"

"Morning, Gloria. You've got it." It was exactly the job she needed for the next and hopefully final step in her evidence against Gary.

She went to the back to put on her lab coat. Gary was at his desk. He looked up at her and winked. "Hi, sexy."

"Morning," she said with as much of a smile as she could manage. The memory of the insincere kisses and embraces she gave Gary flooded over her.

She put on her lab jacket, reached into her purse, took out a little baggie of three nicked Dilaudid tablets, and put them in the pocket.

"Hey, Chris!" Gary shouted. "It's the phone, for you."

As she approached his desk he said, "It's your sister. You didn't tell me you had a sister. Is she as pretty as you?"

Christine swallowed a gulp. "We're very different," she lied as she picked up the receiver.

"Hi, Carolyn," she said into the phone. She tried to control the emotion she was feeling, to keep herself from crying out in front of Gary, "Oh, Carolyn. Please, please don't be mad at me anymore."

"Chris," Carolyn started. "Listen, Bob isn't at school. The whole school is gossiping about how he was arrested on a drug charge.

We've got to go to the state troopers and tell them what happened. We've got to explain it to his parents."

Gary was watching Christine. She had to say something to him so that Carolyn would know he was there.

"Just a sec, Carolyn," she said in an offhanded, careless way as if they'd been talking about what they'd have for dinner. "Gary, do we have lunch break at the same time today?"

"Yeah," he grinned. "We do. Why?"

"Just wondered." Then back into the phone. "Listen, Carolyn, I've got to hurry. The work's backed up here this morning. Why don't you give me your number and I'll call you back later?"

"I don't believe you!" Carolyn almost shouted. Christine pressed the receiver hard against her ear so stray sounds wouldn't leak out. "You're not coming, are you?"

Please, Carolyn, Christine thought. Just give me the number. I'll call you right back.

"Is it that you can't talk because Gary's there?"

"Right," Christine answered.

Finally Carolyn gave her the phone number of the pay phone at school.

"So," Gary said when she'd hung up, "why'd you want to know if we had the same lunch break?" He put his arm around her waist.

She didn't resist his hug and smiled down

at him. "I thought maybe we could go to your place for lunch."

"I'd love to have you for lunch," he answered.

A few minutes later, before she went on the elevator with the control drugs, Christine dialed the number Carolyn had given her. She answered.

"Carolyn, don't say anything, just listen. I know you're mad. I can feel it all over inside me. But you've got to trust me a little longer. And you've got to help me. I need you. I can't do this alone. I'm not going to the troopers with you."

"But —" Carolyn said.

"Just listen," Christine interrupted. "You go and tell them everything. Get them to believe you enough to have a search warrant drawn up and go to Gary's cabin at —" She looked at her watch. "— at twelve-thirty. I'll be there with him and with all the evidence we'll need to expose Gary and clear Bob."

"But Chris —"

"Please. It's the only way."

Carolyn hung up the phone without agreeing. But Christine knew that she'd do it. Because she knew she'd feel and do the same things that Carolyn had been doing if their roles were reversed.

Wouldn't she?

The elevator was empty when it stopped

at the basement level. She rolled on her cart and waited breathlessly for the doors to close. No one else got on. She pressed TWO. Then she quickly opened the narcotics container tray and switched every other Dilaudid tablet with a nicked Dilaudid tablet Bob had bought. This was the final proof. Would the three tablets she had removed, tablets that were going to the floor as Dilaudids, be placebos, substitutes?

Just as she had completed the switch, the elevator stopped at the first floor. Dr. Pisinelli got on and pressed TWO. He was all smiles.

"Well, well. Just the young lady I wanted to see."

"Good morning, Doctor." What's this all about? she wondered.

"You and I are going to pay a visit to Mr. Trono and bring him some good news."

"We are?"

"I just read his X-ray. His leg's healing beautifully. I have no doubts that he will walk as straight and tall as ever. He'll be playing active sports again within a year."

A surge of joy ran through Christine. She was transported. Throwing her arms up in the air she shouted, "That's terrific!" The elevator stopped with a lurch, and three white tablets fell from her hands to the floor.

Pisinelli looked at them, at the control drug cart.

She bent to pick them up, but he beat her to it.

They sat in the palm of his large hand. "Dilaudid," he said to himself as he looked at them. "My patients' Dilaudid!"

"I can explain," she said.

He glared at her. "I'll bet you can! Can you explain it to my patients who haven't been getting the right dosage for their pain so you can have your kicks? How about your own boyfriend? Do you understand what this means to them?"

He inspected a tablet carefully. Crumpled it between his fingers. "A placebo. I see. You were going to substitute these for Dilaudid."

"No. No. Those tablets were in the tray. I suspected — "

The elevator doors opened. Two nurses waited for her to get off with the cart so they could get on.

"I can explain everything," she pleaded with Pisinelli. "I can. You have to give me a chance."

He gave her a little push. "Just get off the elevator."

He led her, cart and all, into a small consultation room and slammed the door behind them. "The cruelty of it. That's what really disturbs me," he started. "Have you ever experienced great pain? You've certainly seen what Joe's been through and you let him suffer needlessly." His face was purple with rage as he marched up and down the room, shouting and glaring at Christine. "I suspected something unethical was going on in the pharmacy, but I never expected anyone working in a medical facility could be so cruel. I guess I hadn't counted on teenagers!"

"You're not even giving me a chance to explain!" Christine screamed as their shouts overlapped. "I'm not the one who's been doing it. I suspected, too. Now we have evidence."

He finally wound down. "Go ahead," he said as he sat on the edge of the conference table and looked at his watch. "You've got two minutes. I'm listening."

She told him everything. How she'd suspected Gary. Her theory about Mrs. Stanley's death. How she'd set Bob up to see if he was given the drugs she marked. "And those placebos," she said. "They were in the Dilaudid tray that Gary prepared for the floor. I took them out and replaced them with the real morphine that Bob bought at school. And Joe. Watching how much he was suffering was what made me suspicious in the first place." She stared at him dead center. "How could you possibly think I'd do such horrible things to people? You don't even know me."

"I'm looking at the evidence. It doesn't fall in your favor."

"Gary Sanders has been stealing drugs. On the hospital end, I think he works alone. And those placebos. . . ." She pointed to the pills that Dr. Pisinelli had put on the table. "... They're the final proof. If you look at the Dilaudid tablets in the first tray, you'll see that three of them have little nicks. They're real Dilaudid. I exchanged them for the pills I was holding when you got on the elevator. I swear to you." She picked up a narcotic container tray and held it out to him.

He took it and picked up six tablets. Three of them had a nick. Each was Dilaudid. "I'm still not sure I believe you," he said.

"I'm not asking you to believe me all the way. Just give me a chance. I've told Gary I wanted to have lunch with him at his cabin. If you could convince the police to come there with a search warrant, they'll find all the proof they need that Gary's a drug dealer. Then I'll tell them everything I told you."

He was silent, thoughtful. He stood up. "Sounds like the perfect getaway plan to me."

"So have us followed," she said. "Just go to the police. Now."

"Or you could be framing your partner," he added.

"Please," Christine begged. "Help me get to the bottom of this."

Finally he agreed to go to the police without her. "Deliver your control drugs as usual," he ordered.

"But there still might be placebos in there," she protested.

"I'll have them all tested today and the stock cleaned up. Whether it's you or someone else that's tampered with them, the State

Drug Inspector will be in here in a matter of hours. I'm reporting this right away."

"Don't forget to tell Joe," she said as they left the conference room.

Pisinelli looked at her questioningly.

"About his leg," she explained. "That he won't limp."

When she got back to the pharmacy, she picked drugs with Gloria. Twice Gary walked by and gave her bottom a tap. She smiled at him over her shoulder.

She was tired, so tired. Tired of the games, of pretending with Gary. But mostly tired from the loss of her twin connection. She was feeling very alone for the first time in her life.

At ten to twelve she went to Gary's desk. "I'm finished," she said. "Ready for lunch?"

He clicked off the computer. "Very ready," he said with a wink.

When they were leaving he called to Gloria, "We're off to lunch, Gloria. We might be a little late getting back, so you just hold the fort."

Christine saw Gloria's face drop. She must think I'm a slut, Christine thought. I hate these lies.

"What're you doing way over there?" Gary asked as they pulled out of the hospital parking lot.

"Using my seat belt," Christine answered

as she gave a tug to the gray over-the-shoulder safety device.

"You're safe with me, baby." He winked. "Come on over."

She clicked the belt in place. "Since my friends were in that car crash on Dug Road I've been a little paranoid about seat belts."

"Have it your way," he answered as they screeched onto Route 41.

Carolyn rushed into the state trooper's office. She'd practically signed her life away (and wasted half an hour) to borrow Linda's car.

"I'm looking for Bob Connell," she said to the young trooper at the front desk.

"If you're not his lawyer or his mother, Miss, you have no business being here."

"But I do," she protested. "I can explain everything. My sister and I, we figured out who's supplying the drugs to kids at school. Bob was just part of a set-up to prove it."

"You've watched too much tv, Miss. This isn't *Hill Street Blues*."

An older trooper came out of the office behind the front-desk rookie.

"You've got to listen to me," she said loudly enough so the senior officer would hear. "I can explain everything. We have evidence, if you'll just go look." She took a deep breath to hold down her panic.

"What's going on here?" the trooper asked. He saw Carolyn. "I tried to tell you nicely last night, young lady," he said as he walked toward her. "You'll be known by the company you keep. Now just get yourself back to school where you belong."

Carolyn yelled, "But you didn't tell me anything last night. That was my sister. My twin."

The trooper looked her up and down. "That's amazing, just amazing. Same looks, same voice, same little gestures."

"Please listen to me. My sister, the one you met, works at the hospital pharmacy." Carolyn went on with a rambling version of what had happened. The troopers were listening — a little amused, a little annoyed, a lot unconvinced.

She was up to "My sister went to his cabin while I took her place on a date with Gary Sanders . . ." when Dr. Pisinelli came storming into the station.

"What are you doing here?" he said to Carolyn. "I believed you enough to come for the police to go to Gary Sanders' place, and you're here. I don't have time to waste, Miss Christine Baird."

"I'm not Christine," Carolyn said for the umpteenth time.

"She's her sister, her twin," the trooper interrupted. With sarcasm.

"This is beginning to sound like a sit-com," the rookie trooper said. "All we need is a laugh track."

"This isn't a comedy," Carolyn said with

great calm, authority, and volume. "And Chris and I aren't some kind of freaks." She stood taller and made them listen on the strength of her conviction. "My sister had the courage to follow through on her suspicions about a transfer of drugs from the hospital to the high school. She's been very upset that patients are being deprived of pain killers. She thinks the theft of drugs from the hospital was responsible for the death of at least one patient. All she's asking you to do is go to Gary Sanders' place and search for drugs. She's getting him to go there right now. Is it such a lot to ask?" She'd never made such a long, impassioned speech in her life.

And Christine had never had such a long, *un*impassioned kiss as she'd just finished with Gary Sanders. Where were the troopers? She didn't know how much longer she could hold Gary off. She pulled away from the kiss. "This isn't the Olympics, Gary. Slow down."

"Hey," he said. "We don't have all day. The drugs are waiting."

I hope so, she thought. I hope they're waiting on the closet floor right where I saw them last night. Then she got the flash thought. What if he's moved them out? They easily could be out of the house and on the street being sold. What if he didn't have any drugs in the house after all?

She had to find out.

She smiled at him. "I have to go to the bathroom."

"You do that an awful lot," he said.

"A girl has to take care of herself," Christine explained as she picked up her purse.

As she went up the stairs she prayed that the bathroom door had a lock on it. That if she had to, she could lock herself in there. Under no circumstances was she about to end her virgin days with Gary Sanders.

In the bedroom she tiptoed over to the closet door. It was locked. Why hadn't it been locked last night?

Then she went into the bathroom. No lock. She peed out of nervousness. As she washed her hands she thought very, very hard. Hurry, Carolyn.

"Hurry, Chris," Gary called from the bedroom. "Lunch hour's half over."

"Coming," she called back.

Did she hear a car pull up?

"Shit," Gary growled. "My roommate must be here. We'll lock the door."

Christine came out. Gary Sanders was lolling on his waterbed — in his underwear.

She couldn't get locked in here with him. Maybe it was his roommate and not the troopers. And even if it was the troopers, she'd be a hostage if he locked the door. She ran out of the room.

"Christ," Gary yelled as he jumped off the bed and ran after her. "I'm sick of your little girl games."

He was chasing down the stairs after her when she opened the door to three state troopers.

Christine moved behind one of the troopers. Gary stood on the stairs in his navy blue jockey shorts.

"Hey, guys," he managed. "What can I do for you?"

"Mr. Gary Sanders?" the trooper asked.

"That's right," Gary said. "I'd love to talk to you, but you can understand, I'd rather do it with my pants on." He started back up the stairs. "Make yourselves comfortable and I'll be right back. You've caught me in a rather awkward position here." He chuckled.

"No," Christine blurted out. "The drugs are in his room."

Gary pretended he didn't hear and moved toward his room as fast as he could without appearing to panic.

"Hold it," the trooper boomed.

Gary kept moving.

"I've got a gun on you, son. Freeze."

Gary froze.

Another officer bounded up the stairs. "Jones will go with you. We have a search warrant here. Don't do anything foolish."

As Gary moved into the bedroom with the officer, Carolyn came in behind Christine. "You girls wait here with Officer Franks," the senior officer ordered. "I'm going up there to have a look around."

Christine grabbed her sister's hand. The connection was there again. The lifeline flowed between them. No matter what happened, she knew that Carolyn was there.

"Look in the closet," Christine yelled. "That's where they were last night. He's locked it."

The bedroom door opened and Gary, back in his jeans and shirt, started down the stairs in front of Officer Jones. The senior officer was behind him with Gary's knapsack slung over his right arm.

"I sure don't know what this is all about," Gary complained. "I mean, she was here last night, she could have planted that stuff."

"But she didn't," Carolyn said.

"What?" Gary looked from Carolyn to Christine to Carolyn. "What's going on?"

"You're under arrest, Mr. Sanders," said the state trooper as he unhooked the handcuffs from his belt. "Listen carefully while I tell you your rights."

"Twins. Shit. What is she — what are they — undercover agents?"

"I have to warn you that anything you say could be used against you," the officer said as he clipped handcuffs on Gary's wrists.

"We'll give you a ride home," Officer Jones said, as they watched the first squad car leave with Gary. "Where do you live?"

"I have to pick up my friend's car at the station," Carolyn said. "And I'd like to see Bob Connell now. I mean, this whole thing proves he's innocent, that he was just trying to help. Right?"

"He's not in jail," Jones said. "He was released in the custody of his parents last night. Didn't you know?"

"Why didn't you tell me?" Carolyn asked, half-angry, half-glad.

"You didn't give us a chance," he replied.

Christine directed Carolyn to the police car. "You better get Linda's car and go right over to his house. Explain everything to his folks."

"You're going to come with me, aren't you?" Carolyn asked.

"No," Christine said as they got into the backseat of the police car. "It's better if you go alone. Bob's seen more than enough of me in the last twenty-four hours." She leaned forward and asked the trooper, "Could you please drop me off at the hospital? I've got to get back to work."

Chapter 11

The rest of the work week was madness for
Christine. Answering questions from the
State Drug Board, from Thompson, from the
police. Explaining the whole thing to Joe.
("You're so gutsy," he said. "I like that.")
And to her mother. "Christine," she said.
"You put yourself, Carolyn, and her young
man in terrible danger. I thank God you're
alright. And I want you to promise me you'll
never do anything like that again. Ever."

On top of all the interviews, she and Gloria
had to do Gary's work in the pharmacy along
with their own.

At five o'clock on Friday Christine went
into Thompson's office. "So," she said as she
took the seat he offered, "today's my last
day. If you'd like I can come in this weekend
and help Gloria out. I know you're short-
handed."

Thompson scowled. "What do you mean,
your last day?"

"I'm only here for a six-week internship,"

she said. "Remember? The six weeks are up today. I go back to my regular high school classes on Monday. If you want I can try to get another intern for you."

His face lightened a little. "Maybe. Until I can get a replacement for Gary. But you know, after what we've just been through I can't be too careful about who works here."

"Do you trust me?" Christine asked.

"Of course I trust you."

"Then trust me to find you someone good. I'll train her myself. On Saturday. How's that sound?"

"Sounds like the best we can do now." Thompson let out a big sigh. "It's just that everyone is getting used to seeing you around here."

Christine smiled when she said, "Once they've met my replacement I don't think they'll even notice I'm gone."

As Christine pulled the car into the hospital parking lot on Saturday morning she asked Carolyn, "Did you remember to tell Bob half-mushroom, half-pepperoni?"

" 'Course I did. He's meeting us in Joe's room at twelve-thirty."

"This is where you park," Christine told her. "Any spot that says STAFF."

"Guess it's back to the old school bus for you," Carolyn said. "School's going to seem pretty dull after this job."

"Maybe not so dull," Christine said as she

turned off the ignition. "Joe will be back to school in another week."

They went into the hospital together.

Pisinelli was on the elevator when the doors opened for them at the main floor.

He smiled at Carolyn. "Good morning, Christine."

Then he saw Christine behind her. "And Carolyn."

He looked from one to the other. "Or is it Carolyn and Christine?" His smile was fading fast.

"I'm Carolyn," Carolyn said.

"And I'm Christine," Christine said. "Carolyn will be the only one of us here after today," she explained. "She's taking over my job for the next six weeks."

"Good," he said as they all faced front and the elevator doors started to close.

"Hold it!" A young doctor squeezed through the doors in the nick of time.

Christine pushed the button for the basement level. "Miss," the young doctor snapped, "that's the basement floor. There are no patients on that floor."

"They work here, Doctor," Pisinelli snapped back. "And we're darn lucky that they do."

Both Christine and Carolyn were laughing with Dr. Pisinelli as they got off the elevator and wished him good day.

"What do you think?" Christine asked as the elevator doors closed behind them.

"I think you and Joe and Bob and I are

going to have a lot of fun together. And that we shouldn't worry about the twin stuff. They've had time to adjust. At least Bob has."

"See," Christine said. "You knew what I was talking about without my telling you. Just like always. I mean, anyone else would have thought I meant, 'What do you think about Dr. Pisinelli? Or the hospital.' But you knew."

"Naturally," Carolyn said.

Christine put her arm through her sister's as they headed down the hall to the pharmacy. "There'll always be something special . . ."

They smiled at one another as they finished the thought together.

". . . between us."

About the Author

A school teacher for seventeen years, Jeanne Betancourt is the award-winning author of *Smile: How to Cope with Braces*. Her other books include *Am I Normal?*, *Dear Diary*, *The Rainbow Kid*, *Puppy Love*, *Turtle Time*, and *The Edge*, which is available as a Point paperback. She is also the author of several screenplays and TV scripts, including *I Want To Go Home* and *Don't Touch*, which were produced as ABC Afterschool Specials.

Jeanne Betancourt lives with her family in New York City and Connecticut.